THE IRRESISTIBLE FORCE

The Marquis took off his snow-covered overcoat and lowered himself next to her by the hearth.

"I did not expect the storm to happen," he said, "but now it has I find it quite an adventure."

"It will not be so enjoyable if we have to stay the night," Nerita replied, then lapsed into a stony silence.

He looked at her quietly. "Do you know how extraordinarily beautiful you are?"

Nerita turned her head to one side.

"That is not a proper way for the Marquis of Wychbold to address his Nursery-governess," she said coldly.

He shot her a look of passion.

"I am not concerned with the Marquis but with a man . . . a man who finds himself in very strange circumstances with a fascinating, intriguing creature . . ."

Bantam Books by Barbara Cartland
Ask your bookseller for the books you have missed

1 The Daring Deception
4 Lessons in Love
6 The Bored Bridegroom
8 The Dangerous Dandy
10 The Wicked Marquis
11 The Castle of Fear
22 A Very Naughty Angel
24 The Devil in Love
25 As Eagles Fly
27 Say Yes, Samantha
28 The Cruel Count
29 The Mask of Love
30 Fire on the Snow
44 The Wild Cry of Love
45 The Blue-Eyed Witch
46 The Incredible Honeymoon
47 A Dream From the Night
48 Conquered by Love
49 Never Laugh at Love
50 The Secret of the Glen
52 Hungry for Love
54 The Dream and the Glory
55 The Taming of Lady
    Lorinda
57 Vote for Love
61 A Rhapsody of Love
62 The Marquis Who
    Hated Women
63 Look, Listen and Love
64 A Duel with Destiny
65 The Curse of the Clan

66 Punishment of a Vixen
67 The Outrageous Lady
68 A Touch of Love
69 The Dragon and the Pearl
70 The Love Pirate
71 The Temptation of Torilla
72 Love and the Loathsome
    Leopard
73 The Naked Battle
74 The Hell-Cat and the King
75 No Escape From Love
76 The Castle Made for Love
77 The Sign of Love
78 The Saint and the Sinner
79 A Fugitive From Love
80 The Twists and Turns of
    Love
81 The Problems of Love
82 Love Leaves at Midnight
83 Magic or Mirage
84 Love Locked In
85 Lord Ravenscar's Revenge
86 The Wild, Unwilling Wife
87 Love, Lords and Lady-birds
88 A Runaway Star
90 A Princess in Distress
91 The Judgment of Love
92 The Race for Love
93 Lovers in Paradise
94 The Irresistible Force

Barbara Cartland's Library of Love series

3 The Knave of Diamonds
4 A Safety Match
6 The Reason Why
7 The Way of an Eagle
8 The Vicissitudes of
    Evangeline
9 The Bars of Iron
10 Man and Maid
11 The Sons of the Sheik
12 Six Days
14 The Great Moment

15 Greatheart
16 The Broad Highway
17 The Sequence
19 Ashes of Desire
20 The Price of Things
21 Tetherstones
22 The Amateur Gentleman
23 His Official Fiancee
24 The Lion Tamer
25 It
26 Freckles

Barbara Cartland's Ancient Wisdom series

2 The House of
    Fulfillment

3 The Romance of Two
    Worlds
4 Black Light

Barbara Cartland
The Irresistible Force

BANTAM BOOKS · TORONTO · NEW YORK · LONDON

THE IRRESISTIBLE FORCE
A Bantam Book / *November 1978*

Bantam Books are published by Bantam Books, Inc. Its trade-
mark, consisting of the words "Bantam Books" and the por-
trayal of a bantam, is registered in the United States Patent
Office and in other countries. Marca Registrada. Bantam
Books, Inc., 666 Fifth Avenue, New York, New York 10019.

PRINTED IN THE UNITED STATES OF AMERICA

Author's Note

Sarah Rachel was born in 1821 and died when she was only thirty-six, in 1858, from consumption.

Her genius as the greatest actress of her time was recognised by the world, and she was able to interpret every side of love—passionate, tender, proud, incestuous, and innocent.

She knew in her own life the love of poets, Princes, and an Emperor. The father of her first illegitimate child was *Comte* Walewski, the grandson of Napoleon Bonaparte.

Railway accidents during the development of the railways were, of course, a hazard of travel. In 1876 a bad collision on the South Western resulted in twelve passengers and a Guard being killed. In a collision in 1880, five passengers, a driver, and a fireman died, and forty-two people were injured.

Fogs were responsible for a number of accidents on all railways; but the London, Brighton, and South Coast Railways, having carried sixty-five million people for twenty-five years, had only two fatal accidents, both in dense fogs. In December 1899 the up-Continental boat-train was run into by the Brighton Express, the driver of which had overrun the signals. Five passengers were killed and a large number injured.

Chapter One

1889

"This means," Lord Dunbarton said in a slow, pompous voice, "that all you will have will be the money left you by your grandmother, approximately one hundred pounds a year, and your jewelry."

There was silence, then in a small voice Nerita asked:

"Is that ... really all?"

"I do not need to remind you, Nerita, that since your father died bankrupt, everything he possessed belongs to his creditors."

"Everything?"

"His houses and their contents, what is left of his fortune, his clothes, and anything else he owned."

"It seems ... unfair," Nerita murmured.

"Unfair!"

For a moment Lord Dunbarton's voice rose, then he continued:

"If you think it unfair, how do you imagine your aunt and I feel? After all, we have a certain position in the Social World, and as head of the family I am appalled—yes, appalled is the right word—at the manner in which your father has discredited us."

"You know Papa did not do so intentionally."

"I should imagine not," Lord Dunbarton replied, "but after all the publicity he evoked, the manner in which he flaunted his huge fortune, to fail in such a manner is a lesson to all men who gamble, whether it is with cards or in stocks and shares."

Nerita was silent, too stunned by what had happened in the last two weeks even to put forward any defence for her father.

Of course he had not meant this tragedy to happen, but in a way it was characteristic of him that he had not faced the music.

Instead he had taken his own life, dramatically, leaving a note of apology to all those who had trusted him, and a special letter for his daughter.

Who could have imagined, who could have thought for one moment, that "Dashing Dunbar," as he was known throughout the world markets, would have a financial crash at a moment when Britain was extremely prosperous?

"When Dunbar's about, all's right with the Empire!"

Nerita had been in Rome when she had been recalled to England by a peremptory telegram which had simply said:

Return home immediately. Urgent. Uncle Henry.

She thought her father must be too ill to communicate with her directly, but long before she arrived white-faced and apprehensive at her uncle's house in Belgrave Square, she had learnt the reason for the summons.

It was hard, almost impossible, to understand that her whole world had fallen about her ears.

She had loved her father and relied on him as only children find security and centre their whole existence on a beloved parent.

After her mother died three years ago they had been very close, but Sir Ralph Dunbar, determined to do the very best for his daughter, had insisted after two years of close relationship that she should finish her education.

"I want you to speak languages perfectly," he said. "As you are well aware, I associate only with the intelligent people in the different countries to which I travel. I want them to admire you, darling, not only for your beauty but also for your brains."

Nerita had therefore gone first to live with a family in Paris. Then, speaking French as easily and perfectly as she spoke English, she had moved to Italy, intending to stay only for six months.

Unfortunately, this year when she should have returned in April for the start of the London Season, her mother's aunt had died and her father had therefore decided that since she was in mourning she should stay in Italy until the autumn.

"There will be winter Balls and we will give one ourselves in the country, as well as entertaining in London," he had said.

He had smiled and added:

"I do not want you to 'leak' out, but to appear in a blaze of glory and confound all those who say young girls are a bore."

This was true enough, Nerita knew, for she had learnt not only from her father and her aunt but from her friends that a well-brought-up young English girl was restricted, chaperoned, and usually sparsely educated.

But because Dashing Dunbar was a cosmopolitan figure, because not only was every door in the Social World open to him in London but also in Paris, Rome, and Berlin, she was to be cosmopolitan too.

There was to be no overworked, underpaid Governess for her who knew little more than her pupils, but Tutors who were each an expert in one particular subject.

More important than anything else was her father and her father's friends, whose conversations were more enlightening and far more interesting than dozens of encyclopaedias could possibly be.

Nerita wanted to please her father, for anything that belonged to Dashing Dunbar must be unique and superlative in every way.

So she had concentrated on polishing herself this last year, as if she were a precious jewel that must shine dazzlingly in the setting he had provided for her.

Now the setting was gone, disappeared overnight, and in circumstances that made her feel agonisingly that if she had been with him she might in some way have prevented the tragedy from happening.

It was not the money she minded losing, but him; the father who had always talked to her as if she were his equal, the father who had prized her as if she were the most precious treasure in his whole collection.

And what a collection he had! Even Queen Victoria had been curious enough to visit their house in Buckinghamshire because she had heard so much about it and could not resist seeing it personally.

Society had for years ignored those who were "in the city," speaking of it as though it were something reprehensible and by which they might be contaminated.

But Dashing Dunbar had changed all that.

He was the second son of the first Lord Dunbarton, who had made a great reputation for himself in India, but the Dunbars as a family went back far in history and it would have been quite impossible for anybody to ignore them easily.

Second sons are proverbially badly provided for, and in fact his father had not returned from India with a great fortune like some of his contemporaries.

The family house in Wiltshire was in disrepair, the estate needed thousands spent on it, and the situation was only slightly reprieved when Henry, the eldest son, married an heiress.

Violet was not a great heiress, but she had enough to ensure that they could play their part in Society, which circled round the Prince and Princess of Wales and which was talked of with awe, envy, and often a great deal of malice.

Henry Dunbar, from the time he had left Eton to when he had become the second Lord Dunbarton, had never done anything wrong.

He was everything that was conventional, sporting and typically English.

It was his younger brother who aspired to heights that he had never dreamt of, and who now had fallen into depths which to him were of the utmost degradation.

For years everything had seemed to be roses in the garden.

Ralph Dunbar with his spectacular success in the financial world was extremely generous, and when he was Knighted, his brother Henry could not speak too highly of him.

It seemed strange to Nerita now to hear the same voice that had almost eulogised over her father condemning him when he was not there to defend himself.

And yet, she asked herself, what defence could her father have offered?

In retrospect, although she did not understand these things, it was very unlike him to have put what he himself would have called "all his eggs in one basket."

But the Mine in South Africa had excited his imagination and the reports on the gold likely to be found there were so glowing, so encouraging, that he had been sure that once it was opened and in full operation he and his friends would make the "killing" of a lifetime.

Werzenstein shares had therefore been introduced onto the market in her father's name, with a Board of Directors which read like a page from *Debrett*.

Everybody trusted Dashing Dunbar, and Nerita had heard her father toasted in Paris and Rome just as he had been in London.

It hardly seemed possible that after such fulsome preliminary findings the seam should have faded out and the whole project crashed so disastrously.

But that was what had happened, and now she was left with a hundred pounds a year, and as her aunt had informed her on her arrival, "a smeared reputation," which made it unlikely that she would ever get married.

"God knows what sort of man would take you on, Nerita," she said in a sharp, peevish tone that had never been heard by her smart friends.

"I am not likely to be thinking of marriage at the moment, Aunt Violet," Nerita said quietly.

"Then you should be!" her aunt snapped. "I cannot think what will happen to you, and to be frank, I have no intention, whatever your uncle may say, of presenting you to Society with this horror attached to you."

"I should not expect you to do so."

"Then you had better talk to your uncle," Lady Dunbarton said. "Of course he is prepared to do the gentlemanly thing for his brother's daughter, but I cannot be expected to work miracles."

"I certainly have no wish at present for social life," Nerita answered.

"Mourning does not last forever," Lady Dunbarton retorted, "and when you are out of black—what then?"

It was, Nerita thought, an unanswerable question.

She was well aware that it would be acutely embarrassing for her aunt to expect those who had suffered by her father's crash even to meet her, let alone to entertain her.

She could remember how enthusiastically they had been ready to do so when she had been in London just before she left for France.

"You need not trouble your head over Nerita, Dunbar," she had heard one of her father's cronies say. "We will give a Ball with all the eligible Beaux to dance attendance on her."

His words had been echoed by a number of ladies who spoke of her as a "poor, motherless child" and who promised her father that they would entertain for her in any way he wished.

This usually meant, Nerita thought with a cynical little smile, that her father would pay, but she was well aware that the right entrée into the Social World was essential, and it would be what her father expected.

He had never allowed her to feel that she must keep quiet and not express opinions of her own until she was grown up.

He had never, when they were together after her mother's death, told her that she was too young to appear at dinner, whomever he was entertaining.

Nerita knew that her Aunt Violet had remonstrated with him, saying that it was ridiculous that a girl should appear in public before she was "out."

But Nerita was not an ordinary girl, and she had learnt that although half-educated, shy, inarticulate daughters were to be found in every grand house in England, things were very different abroad.

French girls were far more polished, and the Russians and Germans studied industriously and always learnt two or three languages perfectly.

"What I find so astonishing," a French *Comtesse* had said reflectively, "is that your empty-headed *jeunes filles* should become politically the most powerful women in the world!"

She had laughed and added:

"They step straight from the School-Room into the Ball-Room and yet by some miracle they become part of the glittering Social World, and I shall never understand why."

Dashing Dunbar had very different ideas for Nerita.

Yet now at the very moment when she should have stepped onto the stage to play the lead he had prepared for her in a play that was to be as dramatic as everything else he did, he was dead and the whole Theatre was in ruins.

"I think, Uncle Henry," Nerita said quietly, "I ought to find something to do."

"Do?" her uncle asked suspiciously. "What do you mean by that?"

"Perhaps I could get employment of some kind."

"Employment?" Lord Dunbarton almost shouted the word. "I have never heard such a ridiculous suggestion! What would people say if I allowed my niece to earn her own living, or rather to try to do so?"

He snorted derisively.

"I cannot imagine that you are qualified to do anything which would bring you in more than a few pence with which to buy hairpins."

It was the scathing way he spoke which made Nerita tighten her lips.

She felt that if she was to live with her aunt and uncle it would be nothing but a living hell.

To be nagged by Aunt Violet, who spoke contemptuously of her father and deprecated everything he had done, would be intolerable.

It would be worse still to be considered an object of pity, of commiseration by those whom she had thought were her friends and who had fawned on her in the past in the same way that they had fawned on her father.

"I will make you a small allowance," her uncle was saying, "and as you will live with us, I should imagine, considering what you already possess, that fifty pounds a year would be quite enough."

He gave a deep sigh and added:

"You will not need many clothes, for as your aunt has pointed out it will be impossible for you to accept any social commitments for a very long time."

"I quite understand that, Uncle Henry," Nerita said, "and thank you for thinking of me. But I shall be able to manage quite well with Grandmama's money, and of course, if it becomes necessary, I can always sell some of my jewelry."

She spoke in a brisk, business-like tone which somehow echoed the way in which her father had spoken at business meetings.

Her uncle, looking at her almost as if he saw her for the first time, realised that she was not only exceptionally lovely but there was also something vividly intelligent about her face which he had not noticed in many other women.

Most of the great beauties with whom he was acquainted were attractive, flirtatious, and very conscious that their job in life was to attract men.

And few of them were foolish enough, for it would have been foolish, to parade their intelligence, even if they had any.

"You spoke rather like your father at that moment," he said. "But let me assure you, Nerita, before you waste time in thinking about it that your place is here in my house and it is quite unnecessary and certainly would be unwise for you to attempt to do anything outside these walls."

He was thinking that later Nerita might take up some charitable enterprise.

He believed the Princess of Wales patronised some organisation concerned with Christian Help for Unfortunate Young Women, or something like that.

He was very vague on the subject, but he was certain such charities were eminently respectable and might provide a place for Nerita.

But not at the moment. Not until all the gossip, the clamour, and the publicity had died down and Dashing Dunbar was well and truly forgotten.

"I am sure," he went on, "that there are ways in which you will be able to help your aunt, and I might even request your services myself."

He spoke half-humourously as if to placate and pacify a child, but he noted a little uncomfortably that there was a stormy look in Nerita's eyes.

As if he sensed that she might be rebellious, he added:

"You must leave everything in my hands. I am your Guardian and I will direct your future in the best way I can."

"Thank you, Uncle Henry."

There was just a pause before Nerita said the words, but then as if she felt that there was nothing to gain in discussing the matter further, she rose to her feet.

"I will go upstairs now and see to my unpacking. One thing is fortunate—that I shall not require any more clothes for a long time!"

She made herself speak lightly and even forced a smile to her lips.

Then as she saw her uncle's rather protruding eyes watching her apprehensively, she added:

"Thank you again, Uncle Henry. You have been very kind."

He had been kind from his own point of view, she thought as she went up the stairs.

But every instinct in her body rebelled at the thought of accepting his kindness, and not only his, but also her Aunt Violet's.

She knew that her aunt, who was interested only in the social life, was not only embarrassed and shocked by what had occurred, but she was also, because she was a woman, triumphant.

Now she could say: "I told you so!" and Nerita knew it was because she had always been jealous that her father had been so much richer than his elder brother.

Her aunt had also envied the fact that as a school-girl she bought her clothes at the most expensive dressmakers and had furs and jewels that made Lady Dunbarton turn green when she looked at them.

Of course they had been in perfect taste, nothing gaudy or flamboyant—collars and cuffs of priceless Russian sable, or a little muff of the very best ermine to match a tippet of the same fur.

There were also jewels that were exactly right for a young girl who was to be a débutante: a string of perfect pearls, worth quite a considerable sum, Nerita thought now, and diamond brooches fashioned in the shapes of butterflies, stars, and even a small lizard.

"I shall look forward to the day," her father had said, "when I can give you a tiara as large as the one I gave to your mother. She always told me she felt like a Queen when she walked in to dinner wearing it."

Nerita had now learnt that her mother's jewels, which were to have become hers, had been swept away with the other things which had gone to meet her father's debts.

These included her horses and the pony and trap which her father had given her the last time she was in London and in which she could drive herself round the Park.

Perhaps most of all she minded losing the books and special small treasures she had collected and to which her father had added at every birthday and Christmas.

Certain pictures had hung in her own Sitting-Room which she had loved and which had tremendous sentimental value for her.

However, her uncle had assured her that there

had been nothing to show that they belonged to her and therefore she had no legal claim to them.

Only her clothes, most of which were now too small for her to wear, had been packed up and sent to Belgrave Square, and the empty spare room next to the one where she was to sleep was piled high with round-topped leather boxes.

"What on earth are we to do with them?" Nerita had asked her maid, Emily.

"Leave it to me, Miss Nerita," Emily had answered. "I'll keep anything that might come in useful and send the rest to an Orphanage or a Home for Poor Children."

"That is a good idea," Nerita had agreed.

Now she learnt from her uncle that Emily was to go.

"You cannot afford a personal maid," he said, "and I am sure your aunt will allow you to use one of the under-housemaids—if it is necessary."

The way he spoke the last words told Nerita that her aunt would consider it quite unnecessary that any girl who could not afford to pay a servant should expect to use one.

It was not, Nerita thought, so much that she minded looking after herself as that she would hate to lose Emily.

Emily had been with her for seven years and she felt that after her father Emily was the person she loved most in the world.

She had hoped when she went downstairs to talk to her uncle in his Study that she would have enough money left to ask for Emily to be allowed to stay with her.

But she knew that even if she offered to pay Emily's wages, her uncle and aunt would begrudge the food they put into her mouth and the roof they provided over her head.

She was quite certain that in her over-positive, rather petulant manner her aunt had said:

"Make quite sure, Henry, that Nerita understands that things have changed. She is now dependent on our charity, and the sooner she realises her real position, the better!"

"I do realise it," Nerita said to herself as she opened her bed-room door.

Emily was, as she had expected, still unpacking the boxes they had brought back with them from Rome.

She rose as Nerita entered and knew from the expression on her face that things were bad, if not worse than she had already anticipated.

"You look done in, Miss Nerita," she said. "Sit yourself down and I'll make you a nice cup of tea."

"No, do not go, Emily. I want to talk to you."

The maid waited, looking at her mistress with the expression of an anxious and fond Nanny.

"It is just as you expected," Nerita said, throwing herself on the bed. "There is Grandmama's money, and nothing else!"

"I was afraid that's how it would be, Miss."

"They will not let me keep you!"

There was silence, and Nerita saw the expression on Emily's face and cried:

"Oh, Emily, that is worse than anything else! How can I bear to lose you? How can we be separated?"

"I was expecting it, really, Miss."

"I would not say anything until I had talked it over with you," Nerita said, "but if I sold my jewelry, and that must fetch quite a lot, then I could pay not only your wages but for your board."

"It wouldn't work, Miss, not with Her Ladyship."

Nerita knew that that was true enough and she paused before she said:

"You will have to help me, Emily."

"In what way?"

"I am not going to stay here. I could not bear it. Aunt Violet has never liked me and she will grind me down until I do something drastic . . . perhaps follow Papa!"

"Now, Miss Nerita, you're not to talk like that! I'll speak no ill of the dead, but the Master had no right to do what he did and you knows it!"

Emily had said this several times before and

Nerita did not answer, but merely following her own train of thought said:

"There must be something I can do. Of course Uncle Henry has forbidden it and said I must stay here and help my aunt, and we both know what that means!"

Emily's lips tightened.

She was thirty-five years of age and had been in several grand houses before she came to maid Nerita. There were few secrets about the Social World of which she was unaware.

She had always been very discreet where Nerita was concerned, treating her more as a precious child than a mistress.

But she had sized up Lady Dunbarton as soon as she saw her and since they had returned to England had not troubled to hide her dislike.

"I suppose, Miss," she said suddenly, "you couldn't suggest going back to stay with those nice people we were with in Rome?"

"I do not think the *Contessa* would want me there permanently, Emily. Things were rather uncomfortable as it was."

The maid had no need to agree aloud that she understood why there had been discomfort.

The young Italian noblemen who were supposed to be courting the *Contessa*'s daughter were all too easily beguiled and infatuated by Nerita, and things had already become rather strained before she received the peremptory telegram instructing her to return home.

Nerita went on thinking.

There was really nobody with whom they had stayed abroad who would be prepared to offer their hospitality for any length of time to a girl who was far too beautiful, but lacking a fortune, to be anything but a disruptive influence or a liability.

"I am convinced I must earn my own living," Nerita said aloud, "and it appears to me, Emily, that the only position suitable would be for me to become a Governess."

"A Governess?" Emily exclaimed.

"Why not?" Nerita asked. "Heaven knows Papa

spent enough money on my education, and I like children, even though I have never attempted to teach one."

"I can't see you as a Governess, Miss, and that's a fact!"

Emily was thinking of the Governesses she had known in her other places of employment, poor scholarly women installed in a room that was considered just a step up from the Nursery.

She was aware that while the Nannies were always loved and made a fuss of in a household, the Governesses were usually hated.

She was not clever enough to find the explanation for this in the fact that Nannies had chosen their career, or their mothers had chosen it for them, from the time that they had gone into the "Big House" as Nurserymaids.

"I always told my girls," one of these mistresses had said to Emily, "that if you get your legs under a good table in a decent house, you'll be all right."

They had been all right.

It was Nanny who ruled the third floor and who was respected by the other members of the staff, but a Governess was a very different "kettle of fish."

No woman ever chose to be a Governess—the career was forced upon her by economic necessity.

They usually came from the lower-middle classes and their fathers were generally impecunious Clergymen, Professors, Solicitors, or Bank Managers. The real spur which forced them into the School-Rooms was the fact that they could not find themselves husbands.

It was a wretched situation, and the task of trying to force learning, of which they had precious little themselves, upon bored, resentful, yawning children was exhausting.

The majority of Governesses had little or no vocational training. They just had to study text-books and hope to keep a lesson or two ahead of their pupils.

Their lives in the big establishments where Emily had been employed had, she thought as she looked back, been very lonely.

They thought they lowered themselves if they became too "pally" with the servants, and there was certainly no company for them in what was known as the "front of the house."

"They are neither, fish, fowl, nor good red herring!" somebody had said once.

Emily had laughed politely, not really understanding. Now she knew it was the truth.

And how could her beloved Miss Nerita be one of those?

"It's impossible, Miss!" she said aloud.

"Then what else is there?" Nerita enquired. "I have no training to do anything else."

Emily sat, thinking, her face wrinkled with the effort, her eyes deeply compassionate.

She loved Nerita as she had never loved anyone in her life except perhaps a young man who had come a-courting her when she was only seventeen.

Her father had sent him packing, and since then there had never been anybody else.

It was sad, because Emily would have been a good wife and a perfect mother. She was instinctively protective, and she wanted to cosset, to cuddle, and to love.

After Emily had served fashionable ladies who could well look after themselves, the twelve-year-old Nerita had appealed to everything that was maternal in her.

"If we could find something we could do together, Miss Nerita," she said aloud, "then don't worry about my wages. I'll stay with you for nothing."

"I do not think Her Ladyship would let you," Nerita answered.

"We knows she won't, so it's no use asking," Emily replied.

"She has always made rude remarks about my having a lady's-maid," Nerita went on, "and having anyone as experienced as you."

She made a little gesture with her hands as she went on:

"Her poor, wretched maid gets cursed every time she does her hair, and she is rude to her simply because she is not as good as you are."

"I wants to stay with you, Miss Nerita, and that's

the truth, but I don't know how it's going to be managed."

"We will think of something," Nerita said. "And whatever Uncle Henry may say, I am not going to stay here!"

"You'll have to, Miss."

"No!"

There was something positive and very determined in the monosyllable which told Emily that Nerita had made up her mind and nothing would change it.

She had lived long enough with the beautiful, clever child who had been acclaimed and fêted wherever she went to know that there was a streak of determination in her that in some ways was very unfeminine.

"You ought to have been a boy, Miss," she had said once to Nerita.

Then she had laughed at the very idea, because Nerita had looked at her with her big grey eyes and she thought that nothing could sound so absurd.

Now as Nerita sat on the bed in the fading light, Emily thought she had never seen anyone so beautiful or so unfitted to earn her own living.

There was something unusual in Nerita's beauty and anyone who saw her immediately concentrated on her large, expressive eyes.

They were so unlike any other woman's that everything else about her paled into insignificance.

She had very white skin, and her fair hair was not the gold of most English beauties but more the fairness of the sky in the very early morning, when there is just a hint of the greyness of the night left behind.

Slim and graceful, which came from organised exercising and riding and from having learnt dancing from the great Professors in Paris and Rome, Nerita had a grace that was very much a part of her beauty, and she moved like a young fawn.

It was not surprising that when dressed with the simplicity and at the same time the elegance that only Worth could achieve, men who saw her were reminded of a Greek goddess.

Emily thought for the first time of the temptations that awaited a Governess.

She had known enough about them in one place where the Governess had been pursued not only by the Master of the house but also by his eldest son.

It had all ended inevitably in tears and with the Governess being sent away without a reference, while the men who had been the cause of all the trouble got off scot-free.

At the time, Emily had thought philosophically that "that was life," but what life could be like for an ordinary Governess and for herself was not anything she could contemplate for Nerita.

"There must be something you could do, Miss," she said now. "Perhaps a job in a Library . . ."

Even as she spoke Emily wondered if Libraries were like shops.

A shop-girl was on such a low level of employment that it would be unthinkable for her or any of her sisters, let alone a lady like Miss Nerita, to serve in one.

There were stories about the way the bosses behaved towards those they employed in their shops and the gruelling hours they had to work, so perhaps in a Library it would be the same, and that would be impossible!

"I tell you what we will do, Emily," Nerita said, getting down off the bed. "Tomorrow we will go to one of those places where one engages servants and see what jobs they have available."

"Do you mean a Domestic Bureau, Miss?"

"Yes, that is the name. I remember our Housekeeper, Mrs. Meredith, telling Papa she was going to London to a Bureau to engage a housemaid after poor old Dawes died."

"I remember that too, Miss," Emily said, "and Jones was a very nice woman."

"Where did Jones come from?"

"I expects it was a Bureau in Mount Street. I went there myself once, but it's not a place for you, Miss Nerita."

"I am not going as myself, stupid!" Nerita replied. "I shall say I have already been a Governess."

"They won't believe that—not without a reference."

"I guessed that that was what you would say," Nerita replied with a smile. "But it will be easy."

"How d'you mean, Miss?" Emily enquired.

"I intend to forge one for myself, just as I am going to forge one for you!"

Emily looked startled, and Nerita explained:

"Nobody is going to welcome you at this moment when they see a reference written in my name, are they?"

Emily did not reply. She had not thought of it before, hoping that she could stay with Nerita.

But she had heard Sir Ralph's death being discussed in the Servants' Hall and she was quite certain that having been employed by him she would not be welcomed at any of the grand houses where she had worked in the past.

Nerita was thinking.

"I remember when I was writing out those invitations for the *Contessa,* I had a whole stock of her writing-paper. I am sure there are some sheets of it left in my blotter."

"I'll go and look, Miss."

Emily went into the next room where the trunks were stacked and after a few moments came back with Nerita's blotter in her hand.

It was a very elaborate affair of green Russian leather with gold corners and with her monogram, also in gold, on the front.

Nerita opened it and found that between the pages of blotting-paper there were half-a-dozen sheets of writing-paper embossed with the address where they had stayed in Rome and surmounted by an elaborate coronet.

"You're never going to forge Her Ladyship's name?" Emily asked in shocked tones.

"There is certainly no time for me to write and ask the *Contessa's* permission to do so," Nerita replied, "and as I have often heard you say, Emily: 'What the eye does not see, the heart does not grieve over.'"

"I didn't mean it in that sense, Miss Nerita."

"Well, references are what we need at the moment, and I am going to write two from the *Contessa*—one for you and one for me."

She paused before adding:

"You have also your references before you came to me. For myself, if they require an additional reference I shall say that I was employed by Grandmama to teach her granddaughter, and as she is dead they will not be able to ask her if it is true."

"You'll get into trouble, Miss, and that's a fact!"

"Then let us hope they will be content with the reference from the *Contessa*," Nerita said.

"Besides," Emily continued, "nobody's going to believe you're old enough to have worked."

"That is where we have to be clever," Nerita said. "I have to look older—much older."

"You are far too pretty, Miss."

Emily blurted out the words and her voice was overly loud because she was so perturbed.

"I expect you are right," Nerita agreed. "I remember hearing Papa talking about some incident that had happened in a house where we were staying. I do not know what it was all about, but he and Mama were arguing. Then he said, 'And she is far too pretty to be a Governess anyway!'"

She spoke reflectively, looking back into the past, and Emily ejaculated:

"There you are, Miss! That's just what I'm saying. You are far too pretty to be a Governess, and nobody's likely to believe you ever were one, so you'll just have to think of something else."

"There is nothing else," Nerita said, "unless you suggest I should be a chorus-girl. They like them to be pretty."

"That is something you'll be only over my dead body, Miss, and make no mistake about it!"

Emily thought that Nerita looked indecisive, and she continued:

"Any more talk of going through a stage-door and I'll speak to your uncle right away!"

"That would be very treacherous of you, Emily, but anyway I feel that the stage is not really for me."

As she spoke she was thinking of all she had heard of the actresses being pursued by gentlemen in top-hats and taken out to supper at Romano's in England, the Café Anglais in Paris, and a dozen Restaurants in Rome in which no Lady ever set foot.

Something fastidious and very young in Nerita shrank from the idea of a life that was so utterly alien to anything her mother had experienced.

It would be a life of which she herself had no knowledge whatsoever, and, telling herself that she lacked courage, she knew that it was not something she dared attempt at the moment.

'I will try being a Governess first,' she thought. 'At least I shall be independent. And I shall have time to consider my future away from Uncle Henry and Aunt Violet.'

At the same time, Nerita was sensible enough to know that Emily was right: she did look too young.

She sat down on the stool in front of the mahogany dressing-table with its triple mirrors attached to it.

She adjusted the two sides so that she could see herself from every angle.

"If you saw me without knowing me," she asked, "how old would you think I am?"

"Eighteen!" Emily said promptly.

"That is untrue," Nerita argued. "Girls of eighteen who have not done all I have done look far younger. Remember Lady Chelmsford's daughter who came out to Rome at Christmas? She looked like a child."

"That was because she was very small and had a baby-face," Emily said. "Although you're quite different, you still look young. And be glad of it! There's a long life ahead of you."

"What sort of life?" Nerita asked bitterly.

Emily did not answer and Nerita returned to the contemplation of her own face.

She put up her hands and dragged back her hair from her forehead and behind her ears.

"Do you remember that English Governess in Paris?" she asked. "The one who was looking after the children of the *Duc* de Valois? She pulled her hair into a hard bun that was stuck with hairpins like a pincushion. I used to wonder how many she put in."

Nerita looked round with a smile.

"Do my hair like that, Emily, and let us see what I look like."

"I'll do nothing of the sort, Miss!" Emily said stoutly. "It's quite useless you having these wild ideas, as you well know!"

"It is not really a wild idea," Nerita protested. "And if we could get a job together, think how wonderful it would be! We would be on our own and it would give us both a chance which we will never have here."

Nerita knew by the expression on Emily's face that despite herself she agreed.

"I will pull back my hair," she went on; "and I know what I want . . . spectacles!"

"Spectacles?" Emily echoed. "There's nothing wrong with your eyesight."

"No, but my eyes look very un-governesslike, and what is more, they attract too much attention. Do you remember when Papa took us to Egypt and I had tinted glasses because the sun was so strong?"

"I've no idea where they are, Miss Nerita," Emily said positively.

"Well, you had better try to find them," Nerita replied, "otherwise I shall spend unnecessary money on buying another pair, and you know as well as I do that we have to save every penny."

Emily made a sound that was half a sigh of exasperation and half a growl of unhappiness.

She disappeared again into the room next door, while Nerita undid her hair from the style in which Emily had skilfully arranged it, and dragging it back from her forehead twisted it into a bun.

It was long, silky hair, which hung well below her

shoulders, and the bun was far larger than that of the Governess whom she remembered. In fact, her hair could quite easily have been arranged in a chignon.

"If I can get a job," Nerita told herself, "I could then look slightly more attractive. I would hate to see myself every day looking like this."

She made a grimace at her own reflection in the mirror and knew that while she was trying to laugh she was perilously near to tears.

Then she told herself that she must look on what was happening to her as a challenge.

That was what her father had told her he felt when he grew up to find that his father could afford to give him only a very small allowance, which meant he could have none of the things he wanted.

"I knew that Henry would have the title, the Estates, and particularly all the money my father would leave when he died," he had told Nerita. "I also knew that this meant I would either have to try to make a career for myself in the Army—in an inferior Regiment, as I would not be able to afford the best—or go into the Church, for which I certainly had no vocation."

"And how did you start to become a millionaire, Papa?"

"I suppose it was a mixture of defiance, determination, and of course good luck," her father had replied. "Luck plays a big part in the lives of all of us, and everything I have done, Nerita, has been a gamble."

He smiled at her and explained:

"It is all part of living—whether you are turning over a card and hoping it is an ace, or seeing the horse you have backed pass the winning-post first."

His voice was serious as he continued:

"Or choosing a share out of thousands of others and believing that that particular company will suddenly become successful, so that the pound you have invested will soon be worth ten, twenty, a hundred times more than its previous value."

"I can see that it is exciting, Papa!" Nerita exclaimed.

"I find it very exciting!" her father answered. "But

it is not quite as easy as it sounds. You have to have a certain instinct, which is difficult to explain."

"Try to explain it to me," Nerita begged.

"I think they call it having a 'sixth sense,'" Sir Ralph replied. "Either you have it or you have not, but I believe it is the greatest blessing that a man can have."

"What about a woman?" Nerita asked.

"For a woman it is different," he answered. "I think most women lack it especially in that they fall in love with cads and bounders. In fact, in my experience they invariably choose the wrong man, which a sixth sense would prevent them from doing."

"Do you think I have a sixth sense, Papa?"

Nerita had only been about twelve years old at the time.

"I am sure you have it, my darling," her father answered laughingly.

He kissed her and said:

"There is one thing which I do not need my 'sixth sense' to tell me, and that is that I know you are going to be very beautiful and that all sorts and types of men will love you, as I do. Together, when the time comes, we will try to pick the right one."

"Somebody I love?" Nerita enquired.

"Of course!" he replied. "But he must also have the right assets."

He suddenly looked serious, then he said:

"You are old enough to realise, my darling, that you will be a very rich young woman, and that creates a number of penalties in itself."

"What sort of penalties?"

"The first is that men will be bemused not only by your lovely face but also by the aura of gold with which you are surrounded."

"And that is wrong?"

"Not wrong, but I would prefer to find a man who would love you if you had not a penny to your name."

He put his arm round her as he added:

"Always remember, darling, that your mother married me when I was comparatively poor and unimportant. She loved me for myself, and that is the way

I want the man who becomes your husband to love you for yourself."

It was true, Nerita thought, looking back. Her mother had adored her father just because he was her man.

She was not particularly interested in what he could buy her, except that she wanted the home in which they lived to be perfect because it pleased him.

The great sadness in her life had been that she could not give her husband the son he wanted, for after Nerita was born the Doctors had said that there could be no more children.

"Your father wanted a son to follow in his footsteps," she had said often to her daughter. "You must always make up to him for what he has missed. You must love him a little more than you would do ordinarily, because there is a gap in his life which you have to fill."

Nerita remembered, and thought now to herself:

'If I were Papa's son instead of his daughter, I would work to win back all the money he lost and pay back every penny that he owed and then people would love and respect his memory.'

Her uncle had made it quite clear that her father's creditors would be very lucky if they received a few shillings to the pound.

She had known as he spoke how her father would have hated to feel that people had suffered because of him.

What she doubted too was that those who had acclaimed and applauded him when he made them money now hated and resented him because he had disappointed them and they thought that their trust in him had been betrayed.

"Why am I not a man?" she asked almost savagely.

Then she heard Emily come into the room behind her.

"I've found them, Miss Nerita," she said, "and a lot of good they'll do you! If you think anyone wants to engage a Governess with bad eyesight, you're mistaken!"

Nerita reached out her hand and Emily gave the spectacles to her.

Her father had bought them in Egypt, and they had large plain lenses which were tinted a rather ugly yellow colour.

She put them on and realised immediately how with her hair drawn back they changed her whole appearance.

She might have looked grotesque, had not the outline of her oval face, the straightness of her small aristocratic nose, and the softness of her curved lips prevented her from being clown-like.

"We shall explain that it is only a temporary affliction," she said airily. "And now, Emily, start looking for the plainest bonnet I own, or remove all the feathers from the one I wore yesterday. If I do not possess a plain enough jacket in which to go to the Bureau, I will have to borrow one of yours."

"The whole thing's nonsensical from beginning to end!" Emily snapped.

"We are not just going to sit here being limp," Nerita replied. "We have to do something, and it is a case, as Papa would have said, of 'nothing ventured—nothing gained.' "

Chapter Two

Nerita and Emily climbed out of the hackney-carriage at the end of Mount Street, and, having paid the driver, they walked towards where Emily had said the Domestic Bureau was situated.

As soon as they were in the street, Nerita took off the heavy veil she had worn on leaving her uncle's house in Belgrave Square so that the servants would not see that she had arranged her hair in a strange manner.

She was aware that they would expect her to be heavily veiled because she was in mourning, and she thought also, somewhat bitterly, that they would know she would not wish to be recognised by any of her former friends.

Now she stopped for a moment outside a shop-window to take the tinted glasses from her handbag and place them on her small nose.

She looked at her reflection in the pane of glass and thought that even her father would have found it difficult to recognise her.

She wore the heavy black mourning that the Italians deemed correct, but Emily had removed all the pretty touches of white and the smart braid which had relieved its sombreness.

She had also taken the black feathers and velvet bows from her bonnet.

Nevertheless, nothing could change the colour of Nerita's hair, or, when she was not wearing spectacles, the sensational beauty of her eyes.

Emily had remonstrated with her from the moment she had decided that they would visit the Bureau.

Over and over again she reiterated that the idea was absurd, that it was impossible for Nerita to leave the Guardianship of her uncle, and that the whole plan of earning her own living was completely crazy.

Nerita had answered that if they could be together everything would be all right, and she knew that gradually Emily began to believe that there was something in what she said, although she still protested.

"Whatever you may think, Miss Nerita, you will never get a job as a Governess dragging me along with you. Governesses are not supposed to be friends with servants."

"Then I will be a Nursery-maid," Nerita retorted, "although I imagine you would then, as a lady's-maid, be too grand to speak to me."

Emily smiled but there was no humour in it.

"That's true enough," she said. "Very stuck-up the lady's-maids consider themselves, and as I expect you knows, Miss Nerita, they're taken in to dinner in precedence according to the importance of their mistresses."

Nerita laughed.

"I had forgotten that," she said. "Poor Emily, as Papa was only an Honourable and a Knight, I suppose you never sat on the right of the Butler."

"Not often, Miss," Emily admitted, "not when we were staying in the houses where there were Dutchesses, Marchionesses, and Countesses all ahead of me!"

Nerita laughed again before saying:

"Perhaps we shall be employed by a Duchess. Then you will be all right."

There was silence for a moment; then Nerita asked:

"Where will I sit at table as a Nursery-maid?"

Emily gave an exclamation.

"You couldn't be friends with me as a Nursery-maid, Miss, but you could as a Nursery-Governess!"

The two looked at each other.

"But of course," Nerita said. "I had forgotten about dear Miss Crewe, whom I had after Nanny left and before Papa engaged Miss Gregory, whom I never liked."

She put her arms round Emily and hugged her.

"You are so clever, Emily! Of course that is the answer to all our problems. And a Nursery-Governess is always young, so that they can play with their young charges."

"Not too young," Emily said warningly.

"How old was Miss Crewe?"

"She was before my time, Miss," Emily answered, "but I imagine about twenty-five or twenty-six."

"Then that is what I will be!" Nerita exclaimed. "Twenty-five, and I will change what I was going to say in my reference to a long eulogy about how good I was with small children."

A little later Emily read her own reference and said:

"You've certainly made me proud of myself, Miss."

"And every word is true!" Nerita cried, a note of sincerity in her voice. "If I could add a postscript, I would say that as far as I am concerned I cannot do without you in my life."

"Oh, Miss!"

Tears came into Emily's eyes and she turned away hastily to hide them.

It was certainly true, Nerita thought, because at the moment all she had left to cling to, talk to, and to understand what she was feeling was Emily.

She had already decided that she hated the house in Belgrave Square and everyone in it.

Although she knew that in his own way her uncle meant to be kind, she was aware that he was embarrassed by her presence, and the voice he assumed when he spoke to her was so unmistakably false that it made her wince.

Readjusting her spectacles, Nerita walked briskly on with Emily, to where there was a sign above an open doorway.

Nerita looked up.

MRS. DALE'S DOMESTIC BUREAU

The notice inside the doorway was more informative:

> *Mrs. Dale provides first-class*
> *experienced servants of every type*
> *for the Aristocracy. Also secretaries,*
> *Major-Domos, Governesses, Nursery-*
> *Governesses, and coachmen.*

Nerita read the notice with a faint air of amusement, then climbed the steep lino-covered stairs to the first floor.

A glass door was emblazoned with Mrs. Dale's name and they entered to find a large room with benches round three walls.

On them were seated a mixed assortment of servants.

At a quick glance Nerita recognised coachmen, grooms, rather fat, buxom women who she suspected were cooks, and nervous-looking young girls with rosy cheeks who were obviously just up from the country and hoping for a position as scullery-maid in some nobleman's house.

She had already been told by Emily that Mrs. Dale sat in an inner office, and she walked toward it and opened the door.

It was a very small office with a high desk, and there was a middle-aged woman, wearing what was quite obviously a red wig over a sharp, somewhat repellent face whose main characteristic was a hard, narrow-lipped mouth.

She looked Emily up and down in a manner which was almost offensive, then glanced towards Nerita.

For a moment her sharpness vanished and Nerita guessed that it was because she felt she had been mistaken and that she was not an applicant for a position but an employer.

"Can I help you?" she asked in a voice that belied the hardness of her appearance.

"I should be most grateful if you could," Nerita

answered in her quiet, cultured voice. "My friend and I are looking for a situation together."

"Together?"

The hardness was back in Mrs. Dale's voice.

"I am a Nursery-Governess," Nerita said, "and my friend, Miss Emily Henson, is an exceedingly experienced lady's-maid."

"Why should you want to be together?"

"We have known each other all our lives and come from the same part of the country."

Mrs. Dale looked as if there might be something reprehensible in this, but, opening a large ledger in front of her, she said in an uncompromising voice:

"You've references, I suppose?"

"Certainly," Nerita replied.

She brought out the one that she had written herself from the *Contessa* da Santa Marco and set it down in front of Mrs. Dale.

She read it and it was obvious that the coronet and the elegant way in which it had been written impressed her, but she made no comment and Nerita after a moment said:

"My friend Miss Henson also has a reference from the *Contessa*."

"Is that the only place where you have worked?" Mrs. Dale asked.

"I was for a short while with Lady Mowbray until she died," Nerita answered, "but my friend has been . . ."

"I suppose she can speak for herself?" Mrs. Dale interrupted.

"Yes, I can, Ma'am," Emily replied, speaking for the first time. "I was with the Marchioness of Londonderry and the Countess de Grey. I've got their references with me."

They evidently impressed Mrs. Dale even more than the *Contessa,* who after all was only a foreigner.

She took the references which Emily held out to her and read them very carefully. Then she said:

"Why did you leave the Countess de Grey?"

"I had to look after my mother, who was ill at

the time. She died, and I then took the position abroad because I wanted to travel."

It was actually Paris where she had gone first to look after Nerita, a position which was certainly very different from that of waiting on one of the most fashionable and exacting beauties in the whole of Society.

"They certainly look satisfactory," Mrs. Dale conceded as if with an effort, "and I'll be frank and say that as far as you're concerned I can find you a place tomorrow."

She turned over several pages of the ledger.

"There is a lady in the very cream of Society who requires a maid who is skilful with hair, and another who wants one who's a good packer and doesn't dislike the sea."

"I want to be with Miss Graham," Emily said stoutly.

Graham was the name that Nerita had chosen, thinking that it sounded Governess-like and respectable.

Mrs. Dale consulted her ledger.

"I see I've one place which requires two domestic staff at this moment."

She spoke as if it was something valuable which she did not want to relinquish. Then as neither Emily nor Nerita spoke, she went on after a moment:

"If I send you to a very important client I hope that you'll not let me down."

"We will do our best," Nerita said confidently.

"It might suit you, Miss Graham," Mrs. Dale said, "since what's requested is a Nursery-Governess for one small boy, aged six. But where your friend's concerned it's not so straightforward."

"Why not?" Nerita enquired.

"The position," Mrs. Dale replied ominously, "calls for a lady's-maid for visiting guests who do not bring their own."

Emily knew that this was a step down from the positions she usually occupied.

A personal lady's-maid was always far more important than a lady's-maid who waited on guests, who were of less consequence and certainly less wealthy.

To all intents and purposes she would be little more than an upper-housemaid.

But to be with Nerita she was prepared to scrub floors or do any other menial task.

"I'm quite prepared to take the position," she said quickly.

"The wages'll not be as high as if you worked for the other ladies I've mentioned," Mrs. Dale said.

She looked Emily over and decided it was a pity that she wanted to tag along with a young Nursery-Governess who would doubtless be dispensed with as soon as the child she was looking after went to school.

Mrs. Dale liked to give satisfaction to her more important clients, and Emily's quiet manner and respectable appearance was exactly that of the sort of servant she liked to place in a good post.

"If you take my advice," she said almost in a confiding manner, "you'll strike out on your own. Friendships can be restricting in one way or another, and if you fall out you'll both suffer—you particularly."

"Thank you, Ma'am," Emily replied, "but I'd like to be with Miss Graham."

"Very well then," Mrs. Dale snapped, obviously annoyed at not having her advice taken. "I can arrange for you both to travel on the nine-thirty from Paddington on Thursday to the house of the Marquis of Wychbold."

Mrs. Dale paused for them to be suitably impressed before she continued:

"Wych Park is one of the largest and most important houses in England. I'll write the address down for you and notify His Lordship's Comptroller, Major Marriott, and you'll be arriving at the Halt, where you'll be met."

She was writing while she talked, and Nerita turned to look at Emily.

Insistently Emily shook her head.

Nerita understood quite clearly that she did not wish to go to Wych Park but she herself had no intention of letting such an opportunity pass.

She was sure that Mrs. Dale was correct in saying

that it was difficult to find a place for two servants who wanted to be together.

"I suppose you've the money for the fare?" Mrs. Dale asked. "It'll be refunded to you by Major Marriott, who'll interview you on arrival. If you're not satisfactory, he'll pay your return fare to London."

She handed to Nerita a card on which she had written the address and her reference. Then she said:

"Do you have to wear those spectacles, Miss Graham?"

"Only for a short while," Nerita replied.

"I should think they'd frighten a small child," Mrs. Dale remarked; "and what's more, get out of black. Few children like black. As the Duchess of Marlborough told me many years ago, it frightens them. Makes them think of crows."

"I understand," Nerita said.

"Well, I hope you'll be satisfactory," Mrs. Dale said in a tone as if she thought it was very doubtful. "If you're not, it'll certainly be difficult to find you another position together. They don't grow on gooseberry bushes!"

"I understand," Nerita replied, "and thank you."

She opened the door and as she did so she heard Mrs. Dale say to Emily:

"I can always accommodate you, so if the position isn't what you like, come and see me on your day off."

"Thank you, Ma'am," Emily answered.

She followed Nerita from the office and they walked quickly across the room where there were now even more servants waiting than there had been before.

As they reached the top of the stairs they stood aside to let a lady who was obviously an employer pass them.

Rustling in silk, with a cape trimmed with fur, she walked by, leaving behind her a whiff of expensive Parisian scent.

She looked proud and rather disagreeable, and it was obviously beneath her dignity to notice the two servants who stood aside for her.

Nerita hurried down the stairs and as Emily joined her she said:

"Now listen, Miss Nerita. We're not going to Wych Park. You must have seen me a-warning you not to accept the position."

"It was that or nothing," Nerita replied. "And what is wrong with Wych Park?"

"It's the Marquis—and it's not the sort of house you should be staying in!"

Nerita laughed.

"I shall not be 'staying' there, Emily, I shall be working there, which is a very different thing."

"*That* might be worse," Emily said gloomily.

"What do you mean by that?"

"Now look, Miss, I've heard of the Marquis—heard of him often enough. When I was with the Countess de Grey she was always trying to inveigle him to her parties. She got him in the end!"

Nerita had heard Emily talk often enough of the Countess de Grey.

She was one of the great beauties of London and her photograph appeared in all the women's magazines, and her portrait, painted by a series of famous artists, invariably appeared year after year in the Royal Academy.

"Who is the most beautiful woman you have ever known, Papa?" Nerita had once asked her father.

"That is a difficult question to answer," her father had replied, "because I have admired so many women of different types of beauty."

He considered the question for a moment as he always considered anything that Nerita asked him, then he said:

"I suppose Lily Langtry was one of the most beautiful when she first came to London and was painted by Millais in her one black gown."

"I heard about that!" Nerita had exclaimed. "She was holding a Jersey lily."

Her father smiled.

"It was in fact a Guernsey lily," he answered, "but she was nicknamed 'The Jersey Lily' and it has stuck to her ever since."

"Who else was beautiful?"

"The Countess de Grey, tall and dark like a proud black swan," her father replied. "She made every other woman look pale."

Nerita had laughed, but afterwards, because she wanted to look like anyone her father admired, she had scrutinised more closely the portraits of the Countess de Grey and listened to people talking about her.

While the men's remarks were admiring, the women spoke disparagingly.

Nerita would have been stupid if she had not realised that there were a number of things to say about the Countess which made their voices fall to a whisper.

Now apparently one of these had been the Marquis of Wychbold.

It was of course easy to learn from Emily that the Countess de Grey, like most of the other Society women, had numerous love-affairs.

Emily had described how infatuated she had been with the Honourable Harry Cust, the younger brother of Lord Brownlow.

Nerita, although she was not particularly interested, had heard of him before.

"He is the lady-killer of the century!" somebody had exclaimed in her hearing, but her father had said:

"One of the most intelligent and charming men I have ever met is Harry Cust. If there were no women in the world he would be Prime Minister, or Viceroy of India."

"Why did you say that about Mr. Cust?" Nerita had asked when they were alone.

"Because he is brilliant," her father replied, "and he is wasting his life philandering with a lot of beautiful creatures without a brain amongst the lot of them!"

It was all fascinating to Nerita.

One of the reasons why she had wanted to come to London for the Season was to meet the men and women about whom everybody talked as if they were gods and goddesses and quite different from mere mortals like herself.

Now she thought with a feeling of depression that

the only thing she would hear about these superior beings was what Emily could tell her.

As they walked along Mount Street she waited for information about the Marquis of Wychbold.

"You listen to me, Miss Nerita, and when you've heard what I've got to say, we'll go back and ask that nasty old woman in the Bureau to find us somewhere else."

"You know as well as I do that she has nowhere else!" Nerita retorted. "What is wrong with the Marquis?"

"I'm not saying there's anything really wrong with him, Miss Nerita. I'm just saying that it's not right for you to be in a house where there's no lady in charge."

"How old is the Marquis?"

"I don't rightly know," Emily replied. "Somewhere about thirty, I imagine. Maybe younger."

"Then why is he not married?"

"He is!"

Nerita stopped in surprise.

"Then what is all the fuss about?" she asked. "And why are you not being lady's-maid to the Marchioness?"

"Because she's not there!" Emily repiled.

"You had better tell me the story from the beginning," Nerita said. "There is no use in making a mystery about it."

"What I hears," Emily began, "is that the Marquis and the Marchioness never got on together."

"Then why did they marry?" Nerita asked, then realised that it was a stupid question.

She was well aware that marriages amongst the nobility were nearly always arranged because they were advantageous to both parties.

"From what I was told," Emily answered, "the Marquis married because he loved the lady, and in defiance of his parents wishes."

"Well, that is unusual!" Nerita exclaimed.

"Half Italian she was, and very beautiful."

"Then why did they not get on?"

"That I don't know, Miss. I just learnt they didn't, and the Marchioness leaves England and asks for a divorce, which His Lordship refuses to give her."

"I suppose he did not want the scandal," Nerita said reflectively.

She knew how shocked her mother and indeed her father had always been by divorce and the publicity it evoked.

"That's right, Miss," Emily agreed, "but long before he became a bachelor again, so to speak, the ladies were after him, and since I've been with you I've heard hundreds of tales of his 'goings-on'!"

Nerita smiled.

She knew that "goings-on" was Emily's description of behaviour she thought reprehensible.

"Then I suppose the child I am to look after is the Marquis's son by the lady who ran away from him."

"That would be right, Miss. It must have been six years ago when I hears of it all happening, but he were chasing round long before that."

It might be reprehensible, Nerita thought, but from all she had learnt of the Social World there was certainly nothing very unusual about it.

The Prince of Wales had set an example of infidelity, which had been followed by everybody in the Royal Circle.

Her father had often laughed at the manner in which Society had veered from the pompous puritanism of Victoria and Albert to the promiscuous behaviour of those who frequented Marlborough House to amuse their son.

Although it would have been considered an appalling breach of taste for a young and innocent girl in the School-Room to know of what was taking place in the Drawing-Rooms frequented by the Prince of Wales, Nerita was so much with her father and mother, and later alone with her father, that she was an exception.

It was not only in England that the Prince of Wales was talked about together with his friends.

In Paris where Sir Ralph Dunbar gave huge luncheons and dinner-parties at the Ritz Hotel, the Prince's friend the Marquis of Hartington, heir to the Dukedom of Devonshire, was known to have been for years the lover of the Duchess of Manchester.

Not only Paris but Rome was aware of a tremendous drama concerning Lord Charles Beresford, one of the Prince's closest friends.

When he was wildly in love with Lady Brooke, he received a letter in which she accused him of infidelity because his forty-year-old wife was pregnant.

Unfortunately, Lady Beresford opened the letter, and caused a scene in which the Prince himself was implicated.

There were half-a-dozen other men, all close friends of the Prince and all belonging to great and noble families, who were always involved in one way or another in love-affairs.

These were the talk of every Smoking-Room and evoked whispered conferences in every Drawing-Room.

Nerita could well understand that the idea of her being associated with such men would frighten Emily, but as far as she was concerned she had the answer.

Because she had asked her father, he had explained to her a long time ago that love-affairs were for older women and never for young girls.

"It would be considered most reprehensible," he had said, "for a gentleman to try to seduce a girl who is not married, and in fact it is not thought 'sporting' to make love to a married woman until she had produced a few sons to carry on her husband's name and inherit his Estates."

"But do people not mind, Papa, when their husbands or their wives are unfaithful?"

Her father considered the question in his usual manner.

"I suppose there are some broken hearts, and men often suffer from wounded pride," he replied, "but in a way it is a kind of game, which is carried on according to the strictest rules, the first being: there shall be no scandal!"

"And no divorce," Nerita added.

"Of course not," her father agreed. "That is the ultimate humiliation, not only to the two parties concerned but also to their families, relatives, and Society as a whole."

He spoke very positively; then he continued:

"The trouble with the men and women of my generation, Nerita, is that they have not enough to do. The men shoot and hunt, fish, and play cards, but they do not use their brains to any great extent, and that is always a mistake."

"And is that the reason why the Prince of Wales . . . ?" Nerita began.

"The Prince has been abominably treated by his mother!" her father interrupted. "He is given no responsibility and he is not even allowed to see the State Papers. It is an outrage! And so he has to fill his life with amusement—and amusement usually means women and gambling!"

Her father had smiled and said:

"I should not be talking to you like this. You are much too young, and yet I feel that you have an intelligence which is lamentably lacking in a great many women twice your age."

"Thank you, Papa. I am trying to understand, but I hope that when I marry I shall not have time, as you put it, for love-affairs and will fill my life with constructive interests."

Her father had smiled very tenderly.

"That is the right attitude, my darling, and I can only pray that your wish will come true. But love is a thing that catches up with us when we least expect it, and even the most experienced philanderer is sometimes swept off his feet!"

"When I marry, I want to fall in love completely and irrevocably," Nerita said.

"That is what I hope will happen," her father replied; "and because you are both beautiful and brainy, I see no reason why you should be disappointed."

She had the feeling, however confidently he spoke, that at the back of his mind he thought it unlikely that she would find the love she sought.

It was because, she told herself, he lived in a world where love meant a very different thing from what she dreamt might happen to her.

The intrigue, the infidelity of one partner to another, the clandestine meetings, assignations at house-parties, all seemed to Nerita rather cheap.

And yet, she asked herself, if everybody did it, was she not asking the impossible in wanting something very different?

In Paris everyone talked of love, but what sort of love? Not anything remotely resembling what she desired.

In Rome, the young Italian noblemen, their dark eyes swimming with emotion and their lips curving over extravagant, poetical compliments, made love seem as commonplace as the moonlight and the music that were inseparable from their race.

But still, that was not what Nerita wanted, and sometimes she thought she was asking fate to give her the moon and the stars and perhaps inevitably she would have to compromise with the second-rate.

Now she said to Emily:

"It is no use working yourself up against going to work for the Marquis of Wychbold. We will try it, and if the whole thing is a failure, then we can just come home with our tails between our legs and say we are sorry, we made a mistake."

"And what'll His Lordship say to that, I'd like to know?"

"Not half as much as Her Ladyship will say!" Nerita replied.

"That's true enough," Emily agreed. "But if your poor father was alive today he would agree that Wych Park isn't the right place for you."

"If Papa were alive we would be with him," Nerita said, a little throb in her voice, "and this would not be happening to either of us."

She pulled off her glasses and put them in her handbag.

"I hate pretending, I hate subterfuge, and I hate not being myself," she said. "But what is the alternative?"

They walked home through the Park because Nerita felt that to move in the crisp October air would somehow clear her mind.

When they reached Belgrave Square and she slipped upstairs to her bed-room, Nerita still felt that everything she had planned was unreal.

She would wake up to find that it had all been part of some terrible nightmare, and her father was alive and they were happy together as they had been in the past.

It was Emily who brought her back to reality with a blunt question.

"If we're going on Thursday, what're you going to take with you?"

"Just the things we will need," Nerita replied. "My plainest gowns, and thank goodness Mrs. Dale said I need not wear mourning."

"It's not respectful to your father to wear anything else," Emily said in a shocked tone.

"Papa would not mind," Nerita replied. "He hated people who mourned and wept. He said to me once: 'I have a complacent regard for death. It is living that counts.'"

Her voice broke on the last words and she said:

"It is living which I find so difficult . . . living without him."

Tears came to her eyes then, and Emily said:

"You're tired. I'll get you a nice cup of tea, and I could do with one myself."

She went from the room and Nerita covered her face with her hands, trying to force herself not to go on crying.

What was the point?

It would only make her head ache, and all the tears in the world would not bring back her father and the comfort of knowing that he was looking after her."

She wondered if he knew what she was doing and whether he approved or disapproved.

She knew he would have understood what she felt about living with her aunt and uncle and the misery her life would be. She could have no friends of her own and had to hide from theirs.

'At least it will be a new experience, Papa,' she said to him in her thoughts. 'You always said experience was very important to one's development.'

It was almost laughable to think that she, who should have been one of the greatest heiresses in the country, was to take a situation as a Nursery-Governess.

However, she would have Emily with her, and if she could force herself to laugh at everything that happened, then perhaps it would be an important experience for her personally.

"We can always leave," Nerita said aloud to reassure herself.

She was saying the same words, or rather: "We can always come back," as they left the house in Belgrave Square early on Thursday morning before her aunt had been called.

Emily had told the other servants that she had found another position and had asked the footman to get her a hackney-carriage.

He had stared in surprise at the large amount of leather trunks that had to be carried down the stairs.

"Are these all yours?" he asked. "What're you taking round with you—the Crown Jewels?"

"All my worldly goods!" Emily laughed. "I'm not leaving them behind to be picked over by the magpies."

"Looks to me as if that's what you are yourself," the footman answered impertinently.

Then his voice died away as Nerita came hurrying down the steps.

"I was awake, Emily dear," she said, "so I thought I would come down and see you off."

"That's real kind of you, Miss Nerita," Emily replied in the manner they had rehearsed, "but I wouldn't like you to trouble yourself."

"There is nothing more depressing than steaming away from a station with no-one to wave good-bye," Nerita said.

She climbed into the hackney-carriage beside Emily and the footman told the driver to go to Paddington Station.

Only when they had driven off did Nerita slip off the black cloak which she was wearing over her blue travelling-costume and remove the black veil from her blue bonnet.

"We will push these in on top in one of the trunks when we get to the station," she said.

"I hopes you'll be warm enough," Emily replied. "It's real chilly today."

"It would not have been wise to wear anything fur-lined," Nerita explained, "for although there is no Lady for the House, some men are quite observant when it comes to clothes."

She was thinking of her father, who had always noticed what she wore, and she thought that perhaps even the Marquis's Comptroller, Major Marriott, might know the difference between real fur and imitation.

She was looking very attractive despite the fact that her hair was pulled back from her ears, and it was Emily who asked:

"You've brought your spectacles with you?"

"Of course," Nerita replied, "but I am hoping I shall not have to wear them for very long, as Mrs. Dale said they might scare the child."

"You could scare the birds in them!" Emily retorted. "And once we are engaged, you can take them off upstairs. But you've to promise me, Miss Nerita, on your word of honour, if you goes to the front of the house, you'll put them on."

"Are you still afraid of the bold, bad Marquis?" Nerita asked. "Forget him. I have told you—I am far too young for his taste."

"How's he to know that, seeing that you lied about your age?"

Nerita laughed with genuine amusement.

"I do not suppose that an Englishman asks for a woman's birth-certificate before he makes love to her. And you know as well as I do that to a Frenchman all women are attractive."

"Now if you talk like that, Miss Nerita, I'm going to turn this carriage about here and now and take you straight back where you belongs!"

"I will behave, Emily, I will really," Nerita promised. "And you know that you are as excited as I am that we are starting off on an adventure together."

"There's nothing exciting about it!" Emily snapped. "And I don't know what Her Ladyship will say when you don't return!"

"I know exactly what she will say," Nerita replied, smiling. " 'Good riddance to bad rubbish!' That is how she thinks of me, Emily, and you know that is the truth."

"It's not polite for me to express what I thinks, Miss Nerita," Emily said with dignity.

Nerita laughed again.

"You are an old humbug, Emily, and I will bet you a thousand pounds to a threepenny bit that Aunt Violet will not make the slightest effort to find out where I have gone."

"Did you leave her a note?" Emily asked.

"I left one for Uncle Henry. I thanked him for all he had done for me and said that I was going to try to earn my own living, but if I failed I would come back and ask his forgiveness if in any way I had upset him."

"That was nice of you," Emily remarked, "and perhaps His Lordship'll understand."

"That he will never do, but at least I feel I have done the right thing," Nerita said. "So we need not have any prickings of conscience, but just make up our minds to enjoy ourselves."

She saw by Emily's expression that she thought this was a forlorn hope. But she was relieved to be away from her uncle and aunt.

She felt too that somehow she was starting a new chapter in her life and leaving behind the past.

She did not want to dwell on her father's failure or on his death. It was all too painful. She wanted to look forward, not back. She wanted to try to reconstruct something out of the ruins in which her life lay at the moment.

She had lain awake last night telling herself that she had to play a part, just as if she were an actress on the stage.

It was no use appearing to condescend, nor even to think that she was Nerita Dunbar, who had been rich, intelligent, and beautiful. She had to be the Nursery-Governess she pretended to be.

She was a young girl who had to earn her living, who was looking after a child simply because there was little else she could do in life, except get married.

"That is not really an alternative where I am concerned," Nerita told herself, "because there is no prospective husband hammering on my door!"

She thought of all the men who had said they wanted to marry her during the last six months, and who she knew would have been dismissed out-of-hand if they had ever spoken to her father of such an aspiration.

She had not taken any of them seriously, but she wondered now what would have happened if she had.

It would be terribly disillusioning to find that once she was penniless they were no longer interested in her.

She supposed that if she had been engaged she would have immediately returned the ring and told the prospective bridegroom that he was free again.

If she had already been married that would have been impossible, and to know that she was an encumbrance instead of an asset would have been a dagger-like blow, had she been in love.

"I am fortunate," she said. "I am fancy-free, and I refuse . . . yes, I refuse . . . to lie down and say that my life is over because of what has happened."

She thought of how her father by sheer determination had made himself a great fortune and had become an international figure welcomed wherever he went.

But then, he had had no stigma attached to him as she had.

At the same time, she was certain that one day dashing Dunbar would be forgotten, or people would talk of him in the vague way in which they always referred to people who were dead.

"Dunbar? I seem to remember the name. Was there not some trouble over money?"

How often had she heard similar words spoken about some friend of her father's?

It seemed impossible that her father, so brilliant, so vividly alive, and so sparkling in intelligence, should disappear into the mists of those who were forgotten.

Again she told herself that that was life and there was no use kicking against it.

"Forget it all! Forget! Forget!"

As she sat with Emily in the Second Class carriage, reserved for ladies only, and they left Paddington

Station, the wheels of the train seemed to be saying beneath her:

"Forget! Forget!"

Nerita Dunbar no longer existed.

She was now Nerita Graham, Nursery-Governess, with no aspirations except to make the child committed to her charge happy and perhaps to teach him a little of her own knowledge and, more important, her philosophy of life.

"Our thoughts make us what we are," her father had said once. "It is not really what we learn but what we think that makes us an educated person."

Nerita had thought this over, then said:

"What we think follows from what we hear, read, and see."

"Exactly!" her father had agreed. "And we absorb what we can of it, until what we think about it becomes part of ourselves."

"I . . . understand," Nerita said, "and that is why our thoughts are so important."

"Yes," he agreed. "Bad thoughts can definitely harm the one who thinks them, just as hatred, which is only intensified thought, often destroys not those whom we hate but rather ourselves."

'I must try not to hate Aunt Violet and all the people who have not tried to get in touch with me now that Papa is dead,' Nerita thought to herself.

There had always been so many people in London who had welcomed her in the past.

One or two of them at least might have enquired whether she was staying with her uncle, or perhaps sent her a kindly message or a letter of sympathy and condolence.

And although it was really too soon to expect it, there had been no letters from Paris or from any other part of Europe where her father had been well known.

'I must not hate them or anyone else,' Nerita thought. 'But it is going to be difficult.'

And beneath her the wheels of the train rumbled on, saying: "Forget! Forget!" as they carried her away to a new life.

Chapter Three

"We have done it!" Nerita whispered to herself excitedly as she was being escorted up the stairs by a Housekeeper wearing a rustling black dress.

The one frightening moment had been when, having arrived at Wych Park, they were shown by an elderly Butler into the Comptroller's Office.

She had been afraid that when they had got so far, Major Marriott might find fault and decide that she at any rate was unsuitable.

Then she and Emily would have to return to London.

But he had turned out to be a middle-aged man with a rather harassed expression, his hair beginning to turn grey.

When the Butler had announced: "Miss Graham, the new Nursery-Governess, Sir, and Miss Henson, the lady's-maid!" he had taken off his spectacles with a weary air and leant back in his chair.

They had walked across the room to his desk and Nerita had thought that it was rather like approaching an awe-inspiring Headmaster.

But instead of scrutinising her closely, as she had rather feared, he merely in a pleasant voice indicated two chairs in front of the desk.

"Sit down," he said, speaking to Nerita. "I understand you and Miss Henson wish to be employed together."

"We have known each other for many years,"

Nerita replied, "and would prefer to be in the same household."

"I see nothing wrong in that," Major Marriott said, "and Mrs. Dale informs me that you are both experienced in your own spheres."

Because she thought it was expected of her, Nerita brought out the reference she had written for herself and handed it to him across the desk.

He put on his spectacles again and read it slowly before he remarked:

"It certainly sounds as if you are experienced with children. Well, you will only have one here to look after—young Lord Burton, who, as I expect you have already been told, is six years old."

"I understood that."

"I am afraid he finds learning difficult and at the moment he can neither read nor write."

Nerita was surprised, but she was really not certain in her own mind how advanced a child of that age was expected to be.

She therefore remained silent, and after a moment Major Marriott said:

"I expect you would like to see your charge immediately, and I am therefore going to suggest that you go upstairs to the Nursery, which will now have to be the School-Room, and get acquainted with young Anthony."

"I should like to do that," Nerita said, making a note of the child's first name.

"I am sure Mrs. Dale has told you what remuneration you will receive," Major Marriott went on in a somewhat vague voice.

Nerita had not been told, but she was anxious to escape being asked any awkward questions and did not wish to prolong the interview.

She therefore said nothing and Major Marriott touched the bell on his desk.

The Butler who had escorted them to the office opened the door.

"Will you take Miss Graham to Mrs. Wilton?" the Major asked.

"Yes, Sir."

Nerita rose and went from the room.

She thought that now she was over the first hurdle at any rate, and she had a chance to look round her.

Before she had left England she had stayed with her father in a great many important and magnificent houses.

He had taken her to Chatsworth to stay with the Duke and Duchess of Devonshire, to Woburn, where the Duke of Bedford lived, and to Burghley, which she had thought fantastic and had imagined no house could be more magnificent.

But even at a glance she thought that Wych Park exceeded them all.

It had been breathtaking as they had come down the drive to see its towers, roofs, turrets, and twisted chimneys silhouetted against the sky.

As they drew nearer the huge grey stone edifice with its perfect proportions and long glittering windows, she had found herself admiring it and longing with an intensity that was agonising for her father to be with her.

He would have been able to describe far better than she could the period of the house, the huge murals in the Hall, and the pictures decorating the carved staircase, which she was sure were all by great masters.

There was however not much time to take in everything, for at the top of the stairs the Housekeeper waited for her, and Nerita knew from long experience that she was exactly the right type of woman to be in control of such a superb house.

A long silver chatelaine hung from her waist, while her face, although dignified, was kindly, as was the gesture with which she held out her hand.

"Welcome to Wych Park, Miss Graham. I hope you will be very happy with us."

"Thank you," Nerita replied.

"Major Marriott has asked me to show you the Nursery," Mrs. Wilton said. "As I expect he explained to you, His young Lordship had a Nanny up until three months ago, but she died."

"He must miss her very much," Nerita said.

"Nurse had grown rather old and crotchety," Mrs.

Wilton replied, "and her place was taken by a Nursery-Governess who started to teach His Lordship a few simple lessons, but unfortunately she left to get married."

It struck Nerita that constant change was always bad for any child and usually made them restless and uncertain of themselves.

They were climbing the staircase which she knew led to the third floor and as they did so she took off her spectacles and put them into her bag.

It was important, she was sure, to make a good impression on her young charge from the moment he first saw her.

As they reached the top landing, Mrs. Wilton, a little breathless from the long climb, paused, and Nerita felt she was to hear something important.

When she got her breath back Mrs. Wilton said in a low voice:

"His Lordship's a dear little boy and we all love him, but I do not need to tell you, Miss Graham, that a child, whatever his age needs a mother."

"Yes, of course," Nerita agreed.

"You will find that things are not always very easy where His Lordship's concerned," Mrs. Wilton continued, "but I've no wish to say too much. You'll soon find out for yourself how things are."

Nerita was listening attentively, and as if Mrs. Wilton was suddenly aware that she had removed her spectacles she exclaimed:

"I hope you'll not think me personal, Miss, but you seem rather young to be earning your own living."

"I am older than I look," Nerita said hastily. "I am obliged to take employment of some sort, and I do understand and like children."

"Then if you're in any difficulty you can rely on me to do my best to help you," Mrs. Wilton said.

She spoke in a manner which made Nerita suspect that she was speaking not only about difficulties with her charge but of other things also.

As if she thought she had said enough, Mrs. Wilton crossed the landing and opened a door.

It led into a large Nursery, and even at first glance

Nerita knew it was so like the Nursery she had had as a child that it gave her a pang of home-sickness.

There was the same brass-topped guard in front of the fire, the same rocking-horse in front of the window, and a screen decorated with Christmas cards and transfers varnished over to give it a sepia-coloured appearance.

And of course there was a cupboard in the corner overflowing with toys of every description.

Seated on the floor, making a castle with square bricks, was a little boy, smaller than she had expected, and beside him, wearing a white cap and apron, was obviously a young housemaid.

The latter rose to her feet as soon as they appeared, and after a moment the child, intent on his building, turned his head.

He gave a little cry of delight, ran towards Mrs. Wilton, and buried his face in her black apron.

"I'se building a castle," he said. "A big castle. Come and see, Willey."

"I would like to see it, Master Anthony," Mrs. Wilton replied, "but I have brought a lady to see you."

The child looked up in surprise, and Nerita put out her hand and said:

"Please show me your castle. I have always wanted to live in one."

He looked at her for a moment, with his head tilted to one side.

She saw that he was a beguiling child, very delicately built, with huge dark eyes and black hair.

There was no doubt, Nerita thought, that he must resemble his mother, because there was a foreign look about him which she was sure, although she had never seen the Marquis, was very un-English.

Anthony regarded her solemnly for a moment, then his face was lit by a flashing smile as he said:

"You can live in my castle if you like."

He danced towards it ahead of the two women.

"The staff usually call him 'Master Anthony' when he is in the Nursery," Mrs. Wilton explained as they followed him. "It prevents him from being confused with his father."

"I think that is a good idea," Nerita replied. "Is he ever called 'Tony'?"

"I doubt if His Lordship would approve," Mrs. Wilton said somewhat repressively.

Anthony was showing them his castle.

"Here's the tower, and there's the big room where the Knights all eat, and I'm going to build a moat all round it."

"That is a very good idea," Nerita said, "and you will have to make a drawbridge so that you can pull it up and your enemies cannot get near you."

"A drawbridge," he repeated. "Like the one in my book!"

"You can leave us now, Rose," Mrs. Wilton said to the housemaid, "and tell the footmen to bring up Miss Graham's luggage."

Rose left the room and Mrs. Wilton crossed to the fireplace to poke the fire, which was already burning brightly, with a long black poker.

"You will find that these rooms get cold in the winter," she said informatively to Nerita, "and you must be very insistent that the menservants bring you up enough coal and logs at the beginning of the day."

"I will certainly do that," Nerita agreed.

"I expect you would like to see your bed-room," Mrs. Wilton went on.

She opened a door and Nerita saw a quite pleasant room with two windows looking out over the front of the house.

Anthony slept next door to her and she noted with satisfaction that both rooms were well furnished and had thick carpets on the floor.

The furniture was painted white and there were plenty of chests-of-drawers and two comfortable chairs in her room.

"The bath-room is just across the passage," Mrs. Wilton said.

"A bath-room!" Nerita exclaimed, remembering how when she was a child she had always had to bathe in front of the fire.

"You will find that Wych Park is very up-to-date, Miss," Mrs. Wilton said. "We have no less than three

bath-rooms in the house—quite American I say it is—
but of course His Lordship and the ladies who stay with
us always bathe in their own bed-chambers."

Nerita knew that her mother would have been horrified at being expected to walk down a passage to a
bath-room, because no lady wished to be seen outside
her bed-room unless she was fully dressed.

"His Lordship has also talked of putting in that
new-fangled electric light," Mrs. Wilton went on. "Personally, I'm quite content with gas and lamps, but then
that's what I've been used to."

"Is His Lordship in residence?" Nerita enquired.

"Yes, he is," Mrs. Wilton replied, but she appeared not to want to say any more.

Nerita hesitated a moment.

"Perhaps you can tell me at what time of the day
he wishes to see his son. Do I take Anthony downstairs, or does His Lordship send someone for
him?"

There was a pause, then Mrs. Wilton said in the
repressed tone she had used before:

"If His Lordship wishes to see Master Anthony he
will certainly send for him, but otherwise you keep him
upstairs in the Nursery where he belongs."

Nerita looked at her in surprise, but Mrs. Wilton
was obviously not inclined to impart any further information.

Then she said quickly, as if glad of the excuse:

"I'll leave you now, Miss Graham, and find out
what's happened to your luggage. Those men are taking a terrible time bringing it upstairs."

She rustled away, and Nerita, taking off her cloak
and bonnet, thought to herself that there was some
mystery here.

It was obvious that while Anthony was provided
with every sort of comfort, his father had little wish to
see him.

It was only as she went to the mirror to see that
her hair was tidy and to think how extremely unbecoming she looked with it pulled back from her forehead and her ears, that she thought to herself once
again:

'We have done it! We have been accepted! I have a job and I am independent of Uncle Henry!'

She felt the relief of it all sweep over her like a wave from the sea.

Then because she could not bear her reflection in the mirror she pulled the hairpins out of the bun at the back of her head and, twisting her hair into a long rope, pinned it instead into a chignon at the back of her head.

"Now I look more human," she said to herself, and went back to the Nursery.

It was not until much later in the evening, after she had put Anthony to bed and had eaten a supper which was quite appetising, that Emily joined her.

She came into the room and Nerita gave a little cry of delight.

"Emily! I was wondering what had happened to you."

Emily shut the door behind her.

"I couldn't get away before, Miss Nerita. There were so many of them telling me what I've to do and I didn't like to seem impatient."

"No, of course not, but we are here, Emily! We have escaped! Is it not wonderful?"

"I'm not going to say too much until I know a great deal more than I know already," Emily said cautiously.

"Do not be so difficult!" Nerita admonished. "Sit down and tell me everything you have discovered."

Emily was looking round the Nursery.

"It's quite comfortable, as Nurseries go, but oh, Miss Nerita, it's not the right place for you!"

"Then what is the right place?" Nerita enquired. "Sitting downstairs in the Drawing-Room with people who have doubtless lost money from Papa's mine and who will be ready to spit at me in consequence?"

"Now don't you go talking like that, Miss Nerita!" Emily said sharply. "It's not like you."

"I am not being bitter or envious," Nerita replied. "I am just facing facts, and quite frankly, Emily, I am very thankful to be here. As I said before we came, it will give me time to think. And my charge is a dear little boy. Do you know what he said to me tonight?"

"What did he say?" Emily asked.

"When I put him to bed he said, 'You're pretty and I like you. I like pretty people.'"

"Well, you've got one admirer, at any rate!"

"His Italian blood certainly comes out in him," Nerita said. "He kept reminding me of all those doe-eyed young men I danced with in Rome."

Emily looked over her shoulder as if she was frightened that they might be overheard. Then she said:

"I've learnt one thing downstairs. His Lordship never sees the little boy."

Nerita looked startled.

"I rather suspected that from something Mrs. Wilton said."

"It's true. The housemaids didn't actually say so in so many words, but I got the impression that he hates the child."

"Poor little Anthony," Nerita said. "It is not his fault that his mother ran away."

She looked at Emily and knew she had a great deal more to tell her.

"Go on!" she prompted. "Tell me! I know you are bursting to do so."

"I've not heard everything as yet," Emily said, "but I was right in thinking that this was not the right house for you to be in, Miss Nerita."

"Why not?" Nerita asked, knowing that Emily would tell her anyway.

"His Lordship entertains all the people your mother would have labelled 'fast'; she would never have let them put a foot through her front door."

"I do not see how that concerns me. They are not likely to come and ask the Nursery-Governess to join them."

"I'll tell you one thing you will do, Miss Nerita, and that is you will lock every door on this floor before you go to bed. Your own door and the door of the Nursery. You'll promise me that's what you'll do, or I'll sleep up here myself!"

Nerita laughed.

"So that is what is worrying you! Oh, Emily, do not be ridiculous! From what you have told me about the Marquis, he has the whole of Society at his feet, and it is very unlikely that he will trouble himself with his own servants, which is after all what I am."

"You're no servant and you'll never be one, Miss. Anyone only has to look at you to realise that."

"There are quite a number of people who have not realised it since we arrived here," Nerita said drily. "Major Marriott accepted me for what I pretended to be and so did Mrs. Wilton. Now stop fussing, Emily! I can take care of myself."

"You're much too young and inexperienced to know what the world's like," Emily said.

"I have a good idea what it is like in big houses because you have told me about it," Nerita replied. "What about that old Duke from whom you had to protect a young housemaid? And the Earl's son who ran away with the Music Teacher?"

"Those stories should be a warning to you, Miss Nerita."

"They are," Nerita replied, "and I shall feel quite piqued if nobody as much as looks at me."

Emily put up her hands in despair and Nerita laughed.

"Trust me, Emily. I have you here, and I promise you that if anyone pays me so much as a fulsome compliment I will come running to you so that you can protect me."

"I don't like this place, and that's a fact!" Emily complained.

"Rubbish!" Nerita replied. "It is magnificent to look at. It is much more comfortable than I expected it to be, and the food is edible. What more could we ask?"

Seeing that Emily was going to expostulate, she added:

"Now stop, Emily. I am trying to make the best of everything and you are only making it worse. Personally, I am thankful for small mercies. Anthony is a dear little boy and Mrs. Wilton is friendly. I am not going to ask anything else of fate at the moment."

She knew that Emily was unconvinced, but at least she made no further protests.

Later when Nerita got into bed she said to herself:

"It might be worse ... very much worse. I am sure Papa would think so if he were here."

* * *

Three days later Nerita was telling herself that she had been very lucky.

Emily had been right in telling her that the Marquis had no interest in his son, although whether he really hated him or not it was impossible for Nerita to know, because she had not yet seen him. Not closely, at any rate.

She and Anthony hung out the Nursery window early in the morning to watch the gentlemen going off hunting.

The season opened on November 1 and the nights were cold while there was often sunshine during the day.

From the third floor of the house they could only see the tops of the riders' high hats, but even so, in their pink coats and white breeches, riding spirited horses, they looked very colourful and made Nerita long to be with them.

She had hunted with her father two years ago with the Pytchley.

Because she had been taught to be an excellent rider, she had enjoyed the long runs over the best hunting-country in the world and had distinguished herself by being on several occasions "in at the kill."

Her father had been proud of her and that had mattered much more than the fact that a great number of people had congratulated her on her courage and her seat on a horse.

She had ridden both in Paris and in Rome but that was what she called "trit-trotting" round the Bois and the *Contessa*'s Estate, and there had been no thrill like a hard run across country with high fences to jump.

"I want to ride a horse," Anthony said as they watched the gentlemen disappearing up the oak-bordered drive.

"Why not?" Nerita enquired. "You should have had a pony by now, at your age."

Dressing him in his outdoor things and taking him by the hand, Nerita had gone down with Anthony to the stables.

She had already found that if she wanted something in the house it was far easier to ask the servants concerned than to bother Major Marriott.

As she walked into the stables, which she saw were as luxurious as the rest of the house, with buildings which in themselves were a delight to the eye, a groom came towards them.

He was a middle-aged man and Nerita said:

"Good-morning! Are you the Head Groom?"

"That Oi be, and ye must be th' new Governess for Master Anthony."

Nerita held out her hand.

"I am Miss Graham, and you are just the person I was looking for."

He seemed surprised, and she explained:

"Master Anthony has expressed a wish to ride. I am rather surprised that he has not done so before now."

"It never crossed me mind," the Head Groom answered, "but if it's in him to ride like his father, he should do well."

"The Marquis is a good rider?"

"Best Oi've ever seen, Miss," the Head Groom answered, "an' His Lordship's forgotten more about horse-flesh than most gent'men learns in a lifetime."

"I am well aware that that is high praise," Nerita said with a smile. "What can you do for His Lordship's son?"

"I want to ride a big horse," Anthony said, speaking up for himself. "A very big one!"

"Ye'll have to start wi' a small one first, Master Anthony," the Head Groom answered. "An' Oi thinks Oi've got the very thing for ye."

He walked towards the end of the stables and Nerita and Anthony followed him.

In a stall there was a small Shetland pony, old, rather fat, and not likely, Nerita thought, to be unmanageable.

"This is perfect!" she said. "But why is it here with nobody to ride it?"

"It don't belong to His Lordship," the Head Groom explained. "There was a lady staying here in summer and she brought her children with her. Two nice little girls they was, and His Lordship said he'd house the pony 'til they came back again."

"Two children!" Nerita exclaimed. "It must have been pleasant for Master Anthony to have some companions."

Even as she spoke she saw the Head Groom's eyes shift, and she realised incredulously that when the children were in the house Anthony had not played with them and certainly had not ridden their pony.

She said nothing more but waited while the groom saddled the Shetland pony and took it out from the stall and into the yard.

Anthony was lifted onto the saddle and as the Head Groom led him up and down he was delighted.

"Faster! Faster!" he kept shouting.

"Ye've to learn to walk before ye can run, M'Lord," the Head Groom said, but he was obviously pleased that the child was so interested.

When Anthony had been riding for about half-an-hour Nerita thought he had had enough.

"Perhaps he could have a ride every day," she said to the Head Groom. "What time would suit you best?"

"Half-after-ten, or eleven, Miss, if that's convenient. His Lordship'll be away by then and Oi can give the young gent'man all me attention. Oi wouldn't like to trust him to one of th' young grooms."

"That is very kind of you," Nerita said.

With some difficulty she persuaded Anthony to dismount, as he wanted to stay on the pony. Finally by bribing him with a promise that he could feed carrots to the other horses, he was lifted down without a scene.

Nerita had already learnt that his tantrums could be quite formidable.

If he did not get his own way immediately, he flew into a passionate rage that was quite awe-inspiring.

One moment he would be all smiles, until like a sudden thunder-storm there would be screams and cries, stamping of feet, and for a few moments he would be quite uncontrollable.

Then the storm would pass and he would be smiling and docile, as if nothing had ever happened to perturb him.

He was in fact so violent at such times that Nerita wondered if she ought to speak to a Doctor about him.

But she was very anxious not to make a fuss so soon after her arrival and so she solved the problem by just leaving him alone until he recovered.

She was sure that the real explanation was that he felt insecure and unloved.

Although the servants all made a fuss over him, what he needed, as Mrs. Wilton had said, was a mother, or at least a father who took some notice of him.

He was demonstrative in a way no ordinary English boy would have been.

He would throw his arms round Nerita's neck, and would run to "Willey," as he called Mrs. Wilton, whenever she entered the Nursery.

"How can the Marquis ignore his son in this un-natural manner?" Nerita asked herself continually.

After walking round the garden they went back to the house, and as it was still quite early in the morning Nerita thought she ought to give Anthony a lesson.

She brought out a picture-book to try to make him learn the names of animals and then to write them down while she guided his hand.

He was soon bored, pushing her away and wanting to play on the floor with his toys.

'I wonder how I can get him to learn the alphabet,

if nothing else?' she thought, then remembered a little jingle she herself had learnt as a child.

"Is there a piano we could have?" she asked Mrs. Wilton later in the day.

"A piano?" the Housekeeper repeated. "There used to be one in the Nursery, but old Nanny said it took up too much room. I wonder what's happened to it."

Nerita explained that it might be easier to teach Anthony through music.

Mrs. Wilton was interested.

"That's certainly an idea, Miss. I'll see what I can do."

An hour later an upright piano which needed a little tuning but otherwise was in excellent shape was carried up the long flight of stairs by several sweating men.

They set it against one of the walls near the window, and as soon as the men had left Nerita sat down to run her fingers over the key-board.

Like everything else, she had been taught music by the best and most expensive Professors, and she was in fact a very accomplished pianist. She had often played to her father and to his guests after dinner.

She chose a gay little ditty that she thought would appeal to a child, and at the first notes Anthony left his toys and came to stand beside her.

"Pretty," he said appreciatively.

"Pretty" was the word with which he described anything he admired. Things and people were "pretty," cakes and flowers were "pretty," and now music was too.

"I want you to sing with me," Nerita said.

She struck the notes and began:

> "*A. B. C. D.*
> *Sing with me.*
> *E. F. G.*
> *And dance with glee.*"

She sang it twice, then she said:
"Now you sing it."

To her surprise, Anthony repeated the letters and the tune correctly.

It was quite extraordinary, Nerita thought an hour later, how quickly he picked up anything that was musical.

Again she told herself that it was his Italian blood, and she thought that he had a surprisingly strong and attractive voice for a small child.

Two days later when they went to Church, she was certain that she was right and Anthony was unmistakably musical.

He had never been to Church before, she discovered.

He was bored during the prayers and fidgeted during the reading of the lessons, but when the village choir sang first the psalms, then the hymns, he joined in, without knowing the words, but merely following them in a way which Nerita felt certain was quite remarkable.

She took him out before the sermon, and all the time they were walking home through the Park he was humming to himself the tune of the last hymn which had been sung in Church.

'Perhaps he is a child prodigy,' she speculated, 'in which case sooner or later he will have to be taught by someone more experienced than I am.'

She had already been told by Mrs. Wilton that if she required any books or anything else for Anthony she had only to ask for them.

Now she was determined that they should send to London for music-albums which would help him. She racked her brains to remember who had composed light tunes which were still good music.

At the same time she realised that despite the luxury in which Anthony lived, the pony he could ride, and the attention she could give him, it was a very lonely life for a child.

"Surely there are some children on the Estate who could share lessons with Master Anthony?" she asked of Mrs. Wilton.

"I don't think His Lordship would like that," Mrs. Wilton replied.

It was the inevitable answer to anything, Nerita knew, that might cross His Lordship's wishes.

She found herself beginning to dislike the Marquis, who, while providing for his child in every material way, was prepared to deny him human love.

By the time she had been a week at Wych Park she found herself insatiably curious about the Marquis, and yet it seemed as if she would never see him, let alone meet him.

Emily was delighted at the way things were and ceased her complaints, and what was more, Nerita was sure she kept any gossip about the Marquis to herself.

This was annoying, as Nerita did not like to lower herself by asking outright what Emily had learnt below-stairs, but occasionally curiosity got the better of her.

"Who is Lady Grantham?" she asked Emily. "I gather she was here in the summer with her children, and although they brought their pony with them, as far as I can make out they never met little Anthony."

Emily pressed her lips together.

"Do stop being so stuffy!" Nerita cried. "If you do not tell me what I want to know, I shall ask somebody else."

Emily did not answer and Nerita went on:

"I think you might consider my feelings occasionally. It is very boring, after all the clever and amusing people I have known in the past, to have no-one to talk to but one small child."

She knew as she spoke that she was making an appeal to Emily which would be impossible for her to resist.

"Lady Grantham," she said, "was His Lordship's close—'friend.'"

There was a perceptible pause before the last word.

"What is wrong with that?" Nerita asked.

"Very infatuated with her he was, they all tell me, but it's on the wane. There's somebody else who's taking her place."

"And who is that?"

"You'll not believe me when I tell you, Miss, but it's an actress!"

Emily sounded so shocked that Nerita laughed.

"So is Mrs. Langtry, and even Princess Alexandra has accepted her."

"It's not what a lady like your mother would expect for a gentleman, to bring an actress into his home," Emily said in a shocked tone.

"I think it depends on the actress," Nerita said. "Who is it that has captivated the Marquis?"

"*Mademoiselle* Désirée Duval," Emily said in a low voice. "A Frenchwoman. Have you heard of her?"

"Indeed I have!" Nerita answered. "The papers are full of her brilliant performances, and the manner in which she has captivated the London public. They have hailed her as the new Sarah Bernhardt."

"She's very like her, from all I hears," Emily said stiffly.

"What do you mean by that?" Nerita asked, then answered her own question:

"Oh, I know ... snake-like ... a female tiger! That is how one of the critics described her. No wonder His Lordship's infatuated!"

"It's not right that you should be under the same roof with such a woman!" Emily said.

"I might as well be in Cairo or New York for all the difference it makes! Tell me more. Have you seen Désirée Duval?"

"Yes, Miss, after she arrived last night we leans over the banister upstairs to watch her go down to dinner, and I'm speaking the truth, cross my heart, when I tell you that above the waist she might as well have had nothing on!"

Poor Emily was so shocked that Nerita could not help laughing until tears came to her eyes.

She had seen pictures of Désirée Duval posing on a tiger-skin and wearing a slinky diaphanous gown which, as Emily had said so disapprovingly, made her appear half-nude.

But the English critics, like the French, had been bowled over by the brilliance of her acting.

She could by herself, they affirmed, portray a whole drama of tragedy and passion.

Nerita remembered reading in one newspaper:

Her attitude, her features, the poses of her head
expressed even more than words the accumulated
hate within her heart. A thirst for vengeance
was proclaimed by her clenched fists and in the
nerves that pulsed beneath the cold immobility
of unplacable resolution.

She could understand how any man would find
such a woman alluring, and she was sure that the
Marquis was only one of many of the gentlemen-about-
town pursuing her with orchids, diamonds, champagne,
and expensive parties.

"Is she really in the house?" she asked excitedly.
"Oh, I must see her!"

"That's impossible Miss, as well you know; and
I'm sorry I told you she was here," Emily said crossly.

Despite Emily's protests, Nerita was determined
that somehow she would have a glimpse of the alluring
creature whom she had read about but had never had
a chance of seeing on the stage.

She was quite certain that had her father been alive
he would have taken her to one of Désirée Duval's
performances, but if she could not see her act she was
determined to see her in the flesh.

It was difficult to know how this could be accomplished, but if Emily could peep over the staircase,
why should she not do the same?

Nerita was determined that when it came to dinner-
time the next day she would make Emily show her
where she could lean over the banister.

It was a lovely crisp morning, with enough frost
to make everything sparkle but not to make the ground
too hard for hunting.

Once again she and Anthony watched the gentlemen ride off in their pink coats, and she wondered if
the much-fêted Désirée Duval resented being left behind.

"Eat up your breakfast, Anthony," she said aloud,
"then we will go to the stables. I think you will be able
to have a longer ride than usual today."

"I want to ride in the Park," Anthony said, pointing to where the horsemen were just disappearing
between the trees.

"Perhaps in a week or two," Nerita promised, "but you have to be very good and try to learn to ride as well as your father."

Anthony was obviously excited at the idea, and Nerita was wondering as they walked down to the stables whether she dared suggest to the groom that now that the little boy was confident in the saddle, she herself might be mounted and lead the pony on a rein.

It was, she admitted, only an excuse for her to ride herself. She found it almost agonising to see the stable filled with magnificent horses and do nothing but pat them.

The Head Groom was waiting with the Shetland pony. He led Anthony up and down the yard, and the child was shouting that he wanted to go faster, when through the archway behind them there came a man and a woman.

Nerita looked round and was frozen where she stood, for she recognised Désirée Duval, swathed in sable, and she was certain that the man accompanying her was the Marquis!

For a moment she could only look at the actress, with her slanting eyes outlined heavily with mascara and her red mouth glowing provocatively in her pale face.

There was the hint of flashing diamonds as she moved her head; then as they came forward Nerita glanced almost indifferently at Miss Duval's companion.

If he was the Marquis, then he was the best-looking man she had ever seen in her life!

Tall, broad-shouldered, very English, with brown hair, and blue eyes which were very much darker than might have been expected, his chin was clear-cut, his mouth firm.

She thought too that he now looked cynical, or was he merely annoyed when he saw who was in the stable-yard?

"Your Lordship!"

The Head Groom was touching his forelock respectfully as he led Anthony on the pony towards his father.

The Marquis's eyes seemed to slide away from the boy and to stare at Nerita.

"Who are you?" he asked.

"I'm the new Nursery-Governess, Nita Graham," Nerita replied, and added as an afterthought: "My Lord."

"The Nursery-Governess? I had no idea that Nurse had left."

"I understand she died, My Lord."

"And you have taken her place."

There was something hostile in the way he spoke and in the way he looked at her, which was perplexing.

"I have been here a little over a week, My Lord."

He was obviously no longer interested.

He put his hand under Désirée Duval's arm and drew her towards the stalls.

"I want to show you the horses I bought last week at Tattersall's," he said. "They are quite outstanding."

"*Mais naturellement,*" Désirée Duval replied. "That is ze right word with which to describe everything here, *et toi aussi, mon cher* Alric."

They walked away and the Head Groom looked at Nerita almost beseechingly.

"I will walk the pony back," she said quickly, taking the leading-rein from his hand and starting towards the pony's stall.

"I not finished! More! More!" Anthony began to shout.

"That will have to be enough for today," Nerita replied calmly.

"More!" Anthony cried stubbornly.

"There will be more tomorrow," Nerita promised.

But as they reached the open stall he began to scream at the top of his voice.

"I want to ride now! Now!"

Nerita merely drew the pony inside and began to take off its bridle, but Anthony clenched both his hands over the front of the saddle and screamed.

Nerita ignored him. She knew it was best to do so when he was in a temper.

Suddenly an angry voice from the doorway asked:
"What the hell is going on?"

She turned from the pony, with the bridle in her
hand, and because the Marquis's voice seemed as over-
powering as his appearance even Anthony's screams
died away.

"I am sorry, My Lord," she answered, "but
Anthony gets in these tempers and the only way to
deal with them is to pay no attention."

"Surely you can have more control over him than
that?" the Marquis asked. "I thought he must have been
kicked by the pony from the row he was making."

"There is nothing wrong with him physically,"
Nerita replied, "but he does have these tantrums."

"With which you are too ineffective to deal com-
petently?"

There was no doubt now that he was speaking in
a contemptuous manner, and instinctively she put
up her chin, resenting his tone of voice.

"I do my best, My Lord, but perhaps you can
suggest a better method than those which I have employed so far?"

She spoke coldly.

At the same time, she saw that Anthony, as if he
knew that something unexpected was taking place,
had ceased screaming and had turned round in the
saddle to look at his father with curious eyes.

"I should have thought," the Marquis said slowly,
"that a good spanking might be more effective."

"I doubt it," Nerita retorted, "but of course if that
is the way Your Lordship wishes to punish your son,
then it is up to you. Personally, I think he needs love,
not violence."

He glared at her in a ferocious manner which she
was quite certain would have terrified any ordinary
Nursery-Governess.

She met his eyes fairly and squarely and for a
moment they looked at each other almost like two
antagonists declaring war.

Then suddenly and surprisingly the Marquis
capitulated.

"I am sure, Miss Graham," he said, "that you are

more experienced in such matters than I am. I am glad the boy is not injured."

As he spoke he turned and walked away, leaving Nerita feeling as if she had just passed through a tempest.

Anthony slid from the saddle to the ground, and as Nerita had told him to do he patted his pony's neck.

"Thank you, Robin, for a very little ride," he said.

"Robin will give you a longer one tomorrow," Nerita promised automatically. "Give him the sugar and we will go back to the house."

Anthony drew the piece of sugar that he carried in the small pocket of his jacket, put it flat in the palm of his hand, and was just about to give it to Robin, when he said:

"Robin did not give me a good ride!"

As he finished speaking he popped the sugar into his own mouth.

"That was greedy and unkind, Anthony!" Nerita reproved him.

"No ride—no sugar!" Anthony replied with his mouth full, then ran out of the stables before Nerita could catch hold of him.

Chapter Four

Mrs. Wilton came into the Nursery where Nerita was playing the piano to Anthony.

He was listening intently and when she paused he cried:

"More! More! More!"

Nerita stopped playing and waited to hear what Mrs. Wilton had come to tell her, but Anthony sprang up to rush to the Housekeeper and put his arms round her.

"Come and listen, Willy," he said. "Pretty music. Come and listen."

"I've not got time now, Master Anthony. I've come to tell Miss Graham something rather exciting."

"What is that?" Nerita enquired.

"I have just been informed," Mrs. Wilton said with an impressive note in her voice, "that *M'mselle* Duval will give a performance for us tonight, and everybody can watch."

"A performance?" Nerita exclaimed. "But where?"

"In our private Theatre, Miss Graham," Mrs. Wilton replied. "But I forgot, I haven't had a chance to show it to you."

"Is there actually a private Theatre here?" Nerita asked wonderingly. "And how exciting that we can see *Mademoiselle*. Does that include me?"

"It does," Mrs. Wilton replied, "and as she wishes to perform early, at six o'clock, I thought Master Anthony could come too."

"But of course!" Nerita exclaimed.

She remembered that Désirée Duval was not only a dramatic actress but also a singer.

"That is thrilling," she went on. "But why at six o'clock?"

"I understand that *M'mselle* never eats before a performance," Mrs. Wilton explained, "and so His Lordship thought it'd be a good idea to have a late dinner. It'll be a very large party. Fifty I believe is the number who'll sit down in the Dining-Room."

"It will certainly be very exciting for me to see *Mademoiselle* Duval," Nerita said. "I have read so much about her, and while as a dramatic actress she has been compared to Sarah Bernhardt and to Rachel, she also has a marvellous singing voice."

"I wouldn't know about such things," Mrs. Wilton replied, "but the household's always delighted when they gets a chance to be entertained in His Lordship's Theatre."

"Does that happen often?" Nerita enquired.

"Perhaps once or twice a year, when His Lordship has actresses and such-like to stay," Mrs. Wilton replied with a touch of superiority in her voice.

Nerita could not help being amused, for she knew that there were no greater snobs than the domestic staff in a nobleman's house.

But it was certainly a treat she had not expected, and not only to see Désirée Duval but to hear her.

She took Anthony up in her arms and kissed him.

"Tonight," she said, "you are going to have an experience which I hope you will remember all your life."

He did not understand, but merely struggled free and going to the piano cried:

"More! Play more!"

"There is no doubt what Master Anthony is going to be when he grows up," Nerita said to Mrs. Wilton. "I am just wondering whether he will be a singer or a composer."

Mrs. Wilton did not answer, and Nerita thought that once again she had touched on what was obviously a forbidden subject.

For the rest of the afternoon she found herself almost counting the minutes until it was nearly six o'clock.

She dressed Anthony in his best, then chose with some care a gown for herself.

She knew that since they were having dinner immediately after the performance, His Lordship's guests would be wearing evening-gowns, but that certainly did not apply to the Nursery-Governess.

She therefore chose a silk afternoon-dress which had been designed for her by Worth when she had been in Paris. It accentuated the whiteness of her skin and the strange grey of her eyes.

It was a young girl's gown and yet it had a sophistication and a *chic* which only Paris could impart.

She wondered if any of the Marquis's guests would recognise the master touch and be curious as to how a Nursery-Governess could afford the almost astronomical cost of such a creation.

Then she told herself that she and Anthony would be sitting with the servants and there would be no question of anyone seeing her.

She was correct in this assumption.

When they entered the Theatre, which had been built at the back of the house in the early 1800s, she found that they were sitting in the front row of a balcony, while His Lordship's guests filled the velvet-covered seats below them.

Emily sat down on the other side of Anthony and Nerita smiled at her across the child and said:

"The Theatre is even more attractive than you told me it would be!"

Emily had already informed her that the Theatre had been added to by one of the Marquis's ancestors who had been infatuated with a Ballerina.

He had persuaded her to leave the Ballet to live with him at Wych Park and dance only for his delight.

The Theatre combined the excellent taste which the Georgians, like the Prince of Wales, had shown in their buildings with the elaborate rococo which the Ballerina had obviously expected as a tribute to her beauty.

The red velvet curtains with a heavy gold fringe, the exquisitely painted ceiling with two huge crystal chandeliers, the footlights concealed by gold carvings, all was an artistic delight which entranced Nerita.

The gardeners had obviously been busy all day bringing in from the huge greenhouses a profusion of hothouse flowers which not only decorated the corners of the stage and the sides of the Auditorium but also scented the air.

'No actress,' Nerita thought to herself, 'could ask for a more perfect setting!'

When the curtain went up it showed a stage-set that had obviously been copied from Wych Park itself and had a fairy-like enchantment.

The designer had depicted the Great Hall and the carved staircase with the scarlet carpets and gold balustrades, and the fretted roof of gold and white supported by gigantic gilt caryatids.

Here again there were flowers piled in great pyramids or arranged in huge china vases that might have been stolen from *The Arabian Nights*.

The lighting was skilfully arranged, and like everybody else Nerita waited breathlessly for the first appearance of Désirée Duval.

While she had been looking round the Theatre, the seats below her had filled with the Marquis's guests.

The women were wearing the most elaborate and beautiful gowns, tiaras glittered on their skilfully arranged hair, and necklaces worth a fortune encircled their swan-like necks.

Nerita did not lean forward to observe them too closely.

She was half-afraid, although she told herself it was very unlikely, that she would see somebody she would recognise or who would recognise her.

Instead she busied herself pointing out to Anthony the beauty of the Theatre, and now as the curtain fell again he asked:

"Is that all? Is it over?"

"No, dearest, it has not yet begun," Nerita replied.

She looked at Emily and enquired:

"What do you think has happened?"

"Temperament, I expects," Emily said disparagingly. "You know what them actresses are like."

Then before Nerita could reply, the curtains parted and the Marquis came in front of them.

He was looking, she thought, in his evening-clothes even more impressive than when she had last seen him.

There was no doubt that whatever she might feel about him personally, he was not only strikingly handsome but also had a commanding presence which would have been difficult for anybody to ignore.

Someone in the seats below him clapped, a little ironically, and the Marquis smiled before he said:

"No, I am not going to perform. I am only here to explain that there has been a slight accident. Will Mrs. Wilton come behind the stage?"

Mrs. Wilton, who was also sitting in the front row of the balcony, rose with a flurry and hurried to obey the summons.

Voices rose all around the Theatre, and it was obvious that they were asking one another what the upset could be and what had happened.

"If it's *M'mselle* who's been hurt," Emily said laconically, "there'll be no performance this evening."

"I do hope she is all right," Nerita exclaimed. "I shall be so disappointed not to see her."

She knew that Emily, if she was honest, was also looking forward to seeing Désirée Duval, but she was still obsessed with the idea that ladies did not consort with actresses and even to be under the same roof with one was in some way degrading.

Nerita, however, had no time to argue with Emily, for Anthony was getting restless and was also tired as it was getting close to his bed-time.

She told him a story which kept him amused for the moment, then a footman came to her side to say:

"His Lordship would be grateful, Miss, if you would come backstage."

Nerita looked at him in sheer astonishment, thinking that he must have made a mistake.

"Are you certain that it is me His Lordship wants?" she asked after a moment.

"Yes, Miss, and you are to hurry!"

There was nothing Nerita could do but ask Emily to look after Anthony and then to follow the footman from the balcony. She was conscious that all the staff— and there were a great number of them—were staring at her in surprise.

She went down a small staircase, then the footman led her not through the Auditorium but up a side-passage which took her directly onto the stage.

As soon as she appeared, the Marquis, who had been standing beside Désirée Duval, came towards her.

Without it occurring to her that it was an impertinence, Nerita stood still and waited for him to reach her.

"As you already know, Miss Graham," the Marquis said, "there has been an accident, and the victim is *Mademoiselle* Duval's accompanist. He has fallen and cut his hand rather badly, and it is therefore impossible for him to play the piano."

He paused before he added:

"Mrs. Wilton tells me that you play well, and I am wondering if it would be possible for you to read *Mademoiselle*'s music?"

He spoke in a way which told Nerita all too clearly that he was quite sure that what he had asked was quite impossible.

Telling herself that she disliked him for the manner in which he behaved towards her and towards Anthony, her chin went up and she replied:

"I am certainly prepared to try to meet *Mademoiselle*'s requirements, My Lord."

The Marquis looked at her for a moment, then he turned towards Désirée Duval, who was watching with an expression of consternation as Mrs. Wilton bandaged the hand of the injured pianist.

"Désirée, this is Miss Graham," the Marquis said. "We are told she is quite an accomplished pianist. She is prepared to try to accompany you."

"*C'est impossible!*" Désirée Duval exclaimed with a shrug of her shoulders, ignoring Nerita as she did so.

"Please let us at least try," the Marquis pleaded.

"Everybody has been looking forward to hearing you, and His Highness has come twenty miles especially to be with us this evening."

Again Désirée Duval shrugged her shoulders, and it was quite obvious that she was convinced that any substitute for her own accompanist would be a fiasco.

"May I make a suggestion?" Nerita asked.

Both the Marquis and *Mademoiselle* Duval looked at her as if they had not expected her to speak.

"If I follow the score," Nerita said, "and the gentleman who is hurt conducts, I shall know not only the tempo but exactly how soft or loud the music should be."

"Of course!" the Marquis exclaimed. "That is an excellent idea!"

Mrs. Wilton had finished bandaging the accompanist's hand and now he held it out, trying to move his fingers as if he thought he might after all be able to play. But it was obvious that the action made him wince with pain.

"*Pardonnez-moi, Mademoiselle*," he said pleadingly to Désirée Duval, and with a faint smile she put a heavily ringed hand on his shoulder.

"*C'est la vie!*"

She raised her slanting, heavily mascaraed eyes to the Marquis and said:

"It ees better we say we are sorry and send ze audience home. They see me perhaps another time."

Nerita saw the Marquis's lips tighten, as if he disliked having his plans upset.

"At least give Miss Graham a chance," he said. "And if, as she suggested, *Monsieur* Lafarge conducts her, surely it would not be too difficult?"

As if *Monsieur* Lafarge was convinced, he burst into an excited flood of French, in which he explained that if *Mademoiselle* performed *Phèdre* first, they could tell if the soft background music was in any way adequate. Then she could sing afterwards.

He obviously did not expect, since he was speaking so rapidly and in a low voice, that Nerita would understand, but she thought to herself that it was a clever suggestion.

Taking Désirée Duval's consent for granted, *Monsieur* turned to Nerita and said in broken English:

"Go on ze stage an' play for the audience while *Mademoiselle* change her gown. Play what you choose. I will join you when *Mademoiselle* ees ready."

It was a test, Nerita knew, and without arguing she moved across the stage behind the curtains to where a white piano which toned in with the rest of the decor had been placed in a corner of the stage.

It too was massed with flowers, making almost a screen in front of the pianist, which Nerita knew was designed to prevent the eyes of the audience from being distracted from the star.

She reached the piano and sat down, realising that it was a magnificent Bechstein and similar to the one she had always played at home.

The music for *Mademoiselle* Duvall's songs had been put ready on the stand in front of her and she looked at it curiously, while she realised that Désirée Duvall had disappeared to change her gown.

Then the Marquis advanced onto the stage.

"I will explain to the audience what has happened," he said to Nerita, then parted the red velvet curtains.

Once again he stepped to the front of the stage, and explained to the waiting audience that the pianist had been injured but a substitute had been found.

But, without rehearsal and never having met *Mademoiselle* before, he was sure that in the circumstances they would be understanding and considerate to the understudy.

'Not a very encouraging build-up!' Nerita thought with a wry smile.

Then she told herself that she would give him a surprise.

She would show him that although she might be an unimportant and obscure Nursery-Governess to the son he disliked, she could play the piano as well as, if not better than, the French accompanist.

Two of her Music Teachers had actually said to her at one time or another that it was a pity that she did not have to earn her own living because with more practise she could easily become a professional.

She had not taken them seriously because it was part of their job to encourage their pupils.

Also, because her father was so rich, she had always thought a little cynically that everything she did was seen through rose-coloured spectacles.

Now, she told herself, she had the chance to prove that the Music Teachers had been right.

Because she knew that the Marquis and doubtless the audience would be expecting to hear something soft, quiet, and soothing, she crashed into the resounding chords of Tchaikovsky's First Piano Concerto.

As the curtain slowly drew back, the melody she produced seemed to fill the Theatre with great waves of sound which echoed down from its painted roof.

Nerita knew as she played that at least one person would be listening to her with rapt attention, and that was Anthony.

She had played this particular piece to him before, but it sounded very different on the magnificent Bechstein from what it did on the upright piano in the low-ceilinged Nursery.

After a few moments the music carried her away and she forgot everything, even her dislike of the Marquis and the doubtless critical audience listening to her.

She played as she would have played for her father, knowing he would thrill as she did to the waves of harmonious sound which seemed to make one's own heart vibrate in unison.

Only as she finished and her hands dropped to her lap, and after a second of astonished silence the applause broke out did she remember that she had an audience.

She did not rise or look into the auditorium. Instead, facing her across the stage she saw the Marquis standing in the wings, and he was clapping his hands not with perfunctory politeness but with an unexpected enthusiasm.

When the curtains fell, *Monsieur* Lafarge came to her side to exclaim:

"Magnifique! And now *Mademoiselle* ees ready."

He turned the pages of the music score, and without speaking Nerita played the soft haunting notes of the music that introduced the Second Act of *Phèdre*.

There was not a great deal for her to play before Désirée Duval came onto the stage, dressed in the flowing skirt and the veil that Phèdre wore traditionally with the double belt of cameos round her waist.

She moved towards the footlights with the slow, deliberate assurance of an actress who is conscious that she holds her audience spellbound without even having to speak.

Yet when she did speak she was everything that Nerita had expected—and so much more.

It was Sarah Bernhardt who had said of the same part ten years earlier, when she had first come to London:

"You will see! I am going to give you my blood—my life—my soul!"

It was what Désirée Duval gave and went on giving.

She wept, she implored, she cried, she suffered and the tears that genuinely flowed from her eyes were burning and bitter.

The arms that she stretched out were arms tense with the cruel longing to embrace, craving for the love that killed her.

She left the audience almost as exhausted as she was herself.

As the curtains fell, Nerita found that her hands were clenched and she felt sure that her own absorption in the peformance had been echoed by everybody in the audience.

It was obvious what they had felt, for there was first a deep silence, as the tragedy which they had seen enacted seemed too awful a reality.

Then as *Mademoiselle* Duval was hidden by the curtains, Nerita saw her put her hand up to her forehead and seemed to sway with exhaustion.

The Marquis was beside her, and with his arm round her he led her away to change.

"It was marvellous! Marvellous!" Nerita said in a voice she hardly recognised as her own.

"Play, *Mademoiselle!* We must break ze tension. Play and breeng everybody back to reality!" *Monsieur* Lafarge implored.

Now at his suggestion Nerita played the light music of Offenbach, which in the Second Empire had taken Paris by storm.

She felt that as her fingers sped over the keyboard they swept away her own tension.

By the time the Marquis signalled from the wings that Désirée Duval was ready, she could hear a little buzz of conversation coming from the other side of the curtains, which told her that the audience was back to normal.

Monsieur Lafarge had been turning over the score and she saw that Désirée Duval intended to follow in the footsteps of Rachel and sing "The Marseillaise" as she had sung her way to fame in the Revolution of 1848.

Softly, very quietly, in contrast to the way she had been playing before, Nerita began the music to which all Paris had marched and sung.

As she did so, Désirée Duval came onto the stage, tall and erect in a long white tunic, the figure of Liberty inspired by a bas-relief on the Arc de Triomphe.

In some extraordinary manner, before she even opened her mouth the audience shuddered as she made her entrance.

Désirée Duval's face was a mask of livid pallor, with a dark look of suffering and revolt. Her brows were knitted together, her down-drawn lips contained a storm of threats, and her nostrils were passionately dilated as if they would inhale the fresh air of freedom after the fetid atmosphere of a prison.

To everybody watching, it seemed as if the goddess Nemesis was suddenly freeing herself out from a block of Grecian marble. Then in a voice of anger, harshly and monotonously she began the first stanza:

"*Allons, enfants de la Patrie . . . !*"

She did not sing, nor did she recite. It was a declaration, in the manner of intonations in ancient times,

and at first the verse was sometimes pedestrian, sometimes winged, a strange music which seemed to pulsate
in the nerves of those who listened.

Then, after the cumulative hate and the thirst for
vengeance, she became tender. She melted to tears at
the sacred thought of her country. She knelt to the
tricolour folds of the symbolic flag!

Then suddenly, as if inspired by unseen forces,
she stood and sang "The Marseillaise" with the voice
of an angel.

As Nerita played, following the conducting of
Monsieur Lafarge, she was at the same time an in-
trinsic part of Désirée Duval.

The tears were running down her cheeks, as
nobody could listen and not be moved to the very
depths of their being.

It was magnificent! It was inspiring. It swept even
the most bored and blasé of the audience to their feet
in a frenzy of wild enthusiasm.

As the curtain fell and then rose again, the bravos,
applause, and stamping of feet vibrated like thunder
through the small Theatre.

The audience, Nerita knew, could have sat all
night listening and like Anthony wanting more. But
Désirée Duval was too experienced an actress to try
to do better than the sublime.

She took a dozen curtain-calls, bouquets of flowers
appeared as if by magic, and she carried a huge sheaf
of orchids which Nerita thought must have been pre-
sented to her by the Marquis.

Then at the last call she made a gesture with her
hand in the direction of the piano.

"Rise, *Mademoiselle!*" *Monsieur* Lafarge whispered to Nerita.

Because she felt it would seem coy and rather
foolish not to, Nerita did as she was told.

But when she would have sat down again, to her
surprise Désirée Duval walked forward to draw her
by the hand from behind the piano and present her to
the audience.

Nerita curtseyed to the applause, the curtain fell,
and as the Marquis joined them Désirée Duval said:

"You are good! Very good, *ma chère!* Come with me to Paris and you shall play for me at the Théâtre de Comédie Français."

"You are very kind," Nerita murmured, "and may I say, *Mademoiselle,* it is the most exciting evening I have ever spent in my whole life!"

The Frenchwoman smiled at her; then, linking her arm through the Marquis's, she said to him:

"I must rest for a leetle while before dinner, but eet was sensational, *n'est-ce pas?*"

"A great sensation!" the Marquis replied. "And thank you Miss Graham."

As he spoke he turned away to lead Désirée Duval to her dressing-room, and Nerita thanked *Monsieur* Lafarge.

As she did so, she saw that he was looking tired and old. She felt that the way Désirée Duval had ignored him was cruel and hurtful.

He was afraid for his job!

She thanked him again, then walked across the stage to the passage which she knew would take her back to the house without having to pass through the Auditorium.

She caught up with Emily and Anthony halfway up a side-staircase which was not used by the Marquis's guests.

Anthony looked tired and she picked him up.

"Pretty music! Very pretty!" he said, putting his arms round her neck.

Emily made no comment and Nerita knew only too well what she was feeling.

Only when they reached the Nursery and were out of hearing of the other servants, who were dispersing to their various departments, did Emily say:

"Let's hope there wasn't anyone there tonight, Miss Nerita, who'll inform Her Ladyship where you're to be found!"

"I thought of that myself," Nerita answered, "but I do not think it is likely. I am sure Aunt Violet's friends do not expect to see me and would therefore not have recognised me."

"One never knows," Emily said gloomily.

"Well, whatever happens, I shall always be proud that I played for Désirée Duval," Nerita said. "She is a great *artiste!*"

Emily did not reply, and Nerita thought how startled and horrified she would be if she told her what Désirée Duval had said about going with her to Paris.

She was sure, however, that she had said it just out of politeness and the remark was not in any way to be taken seriously. Even if it were serious, Nerita told herself, she would not go.

It would be too frightening to be alone in the glittering Capital, where everybody was seeking entertainment and of course love.

"I am safe where I am," Nerita said to herself, only hoping that it was the truth.

* * *

The next day everything seemed a little flat after the excitement of the night before.

It was Emily who informed Nerita, early in the morning, that the house-party was dispersing and *Mademoiselle* Duval was leaving for Paris.

"Is the Marquis going with her?" Nerita enquired.

"No, because another party will be arriving for the weekend," Emily replied. "That is, if they can get through."

Nerita knew she was referring to the weather. It had snowed heavily during the night and Wych Park and its gardens looked very lovely under a thick carpet of snow.

The sun was shining and Nerita thought it would be fun for Anthony to make a snow-man.

"Come along," she said. "We will go out and make a snow-man far bigger than you are, and we will see if we can find an old hat to put on his head and a pipe to put in his mouth."

"Too cold to go out," Anthony said. "Play pretty music."

"We will do that when it is dark," Nerita replied, "but first you must have some fresh air."

"Too cold!" Anthony repeated.

Nerita thought it was very un-English of him not to want, like other boys, to go snow-balling, but she ignored his protests, buttoned him into his gaitors, wrapped him up warmly, and took him downstairs and out into the white garden.

She found, a little to her consternation, that the only garment she had to wear that was warm enough was a very expensive fur coat which her father had given her the previous winter.

It was most unsuitable, she thought, for a Nursery-Governess, but without it she would doubtless catch a chill, and she only hoped that nobody would see her.

She walked Anthony away from the house, and, finding a secluded part of the lawns, she tried to create some enthusiasm in him for rolling the snow into a great ball for the snow-man's body, then a smaller one for his head.

She soon realised that Anthony was unimpressed and disliked the melting snow wetting his gloves.

In fact, with his large dark eyes, pink nose, and pale face he looked very unlike the red-cheeked boys whom Nerita had known in her childhood and who were unerring shots when they pelted her with snow-balls.

At last she gave up the hopeless task and said:

"Let us go and feed Robin before luncheon, and perhaps if the snow is not too deep you will be able to ride this afternoon."

Anthony cheered up at once and they set off towards the stables.

Only when they reached them did Nerita realise that the Head Groom was not waiting for them as usual but was busy going round the stalls with the Marquis.

Once she saw that he was there, Nerita would have retreated despite the fact that she was sure Anthony would protest noisily at being taken away without seeing Robin.

But the Marquis looked round and walked towards them.

"Good-morning, Miss Graham!"

"Good-morning, My Lord."

She saw that his eyes were flickering over her and she was instantly conscious of her expensive coat and the hood of the same fur which framed her face.

Then she told herself it was none of his business. As a Nursery-Governess she was not expected to wear a uniform and her clothes were her own affair.

"I want to thank you, Miss Graham," the Marquis said, "for the magnificent manner in which you stepped into the breach last night."

As he spoke, Anthony darted away in the direction of Robin's stall, and they stood alone in the centre of the yard.

"There is no need to thank me, My Lord," Nerita answered. "It was a very great privilege to play for *Mademoiselle* Duval, which I shall never forget."

"I have never known her to perform better," the Marquis said. "I am sure that you also should be congratulated on that account."

"Thank you."

Nerita looked up at him as she spoke and her eyes met his, and somehow it was hard to look away.

Then hastily, as if he too was conscious that something strange was happening, he said:

"I was thinking of going out in a sleigh this afternoon. It is something I have not done for several years. I wonder if you would like to come with me?"

"I am sure Anthony would enjoy it very much, My Lord," Nerita replied.

Even as she spoke she had the strange feeling that the Marquis had forgotten Anthony and the invitation had been intended only for her.

Then she told herself that she was being absurd.

The Marquis looked up at the sky.

"As the sun may not last," he said, "I think we would be wise to start early. Shall we say at one forty-five?"

"I will bring Anthony down to the Hall at that hour," Nerita replied.

She moved away as she spoke, conscious as she

hurried towards Robin's stall that the Marquis was still standing where she had left him in the centre of the yard.

They had luncheon early, and it was impossible, however much Nerita told herself that she disapproved of the Marquis for his behaviour towards his son, not to feel that something unprecedented was happening in that they were going out together.

For this afternoon at least Anthony would be with his father, whatever motives the Marquis might have had in inviting them.

"I want to ride Robin," Anthony said somewhat truculently as they ate.

"This afternoon we are going to drive in a sleigh," Nerita replied. "If you have not been in one before, it is very exciting. It is what Father Christmas uses when he brings the presents to fill your stocking."

"A sleigh with a reindeer?" Anthony enquired.

"I am afraid there are no reindeer at Wych Park," Nerita answered, "but there will be two horses and they will go very fast over the snow."

She felt that the small boy thought it would be a poor performance without the traditional reindeer.

Nevertheless, he stopped complaining that he was not to be allowed to ride, and once again Nerita wrapped him as warmly as she could, hoping that the Marquis would not realise how much his son disliked the cold and how he seemed to be peculiarly sensitive to it.

"There is sure to be a hot foot-rest in the sleigh," she told herself consolingly, "and if Anthony sits between me and his father, he will keep warm."

She knew there were plenty of rugs downstairs, but nevertheless as a precaution she carried an extra one, which she decided she would wrap round the small boy so that there would be no draught round his legs.

She had nothing she could wear except her fur coat, and once again she thought that if the Marquis was surprised by its luxurious appearance, he would at least be too polite, or perhaps too indifferent, to comment on it.

As she walked down the Grand Staircase, which she had not used since she had first arrived at Wych Park, she thought she had been foolish not to suggest that she should take Anthony round the huge house and explain to him the beauty of many of its treasures.

The flags on the walls would be a far better history lesson than anything she could give him. Later on, pictures depicting mythology or the Holy Family could all be part of his education.

"As soon as the Marquis goes away," she told herself, "I will explore the whole house."

With or without Anthony, that was something she was determined to do.

When they were halfway down the staircase she saw the Marquis waiting for them. With his top-hat at an angle and with a smartly cut overcoat, she thought that however he behaved, however unpredictable he might be where his child was concerned, Wych Park was certainly a fitting setting for him.

'But it also needs a mistress,' she thought.

She wondered as she had already wondered many times before what had gone wrong with his marriage to the beautiful half-Italian wife who had run away to leave a lonely little boy behind her.

"I see you are prepared for every emergency," the Marquis said with a look at the rug which Nerita carried over her arm.

"I do not want Anthony to get cold," she replied.

"It would certainly be very unbecoming," the Marquis said.

He was looking not at his son but at her.

She suddenly remembered almost guiltily that she had promised Emily before they came to Wych Park that if she ever went to the "front of the house" she would wear her spectacles.

Because she had not seen the Marquis for the first week she had completely forgotten the necessity of being incognito and pretending to be older than she was.

Now her eyes fell before the Marquis's, and her eye-lashes, which curved upwards at the tips, were silhouetted against the whiteness of her skin.

He looked at her for a moment, then they both moved towards the open door.

A carpet was already laid on the steps and they walked down to where the sleigh was waiting for them.

It was a very pretty sleigh, and different from what Nerita had expected, for it was painted in brilliant colours and she recognised it as being Bavarian.

She knew that it must have come originally from that delightful country where native craftsmen painted and carved so cleverly.

A footman helped her in and as she had planned she sat Anthony between herself and the Marquis, but as he stepped into the driving-seat he said:

"Let the child sit on the outside. It will be easier for him to see what is happening from there."

Nerita wanted to protest, but obediently she moved into the centre, while Anthony sat where she had intended to sit.

He was quite happy as he leant over the side and watched the sleigh moving over the snow.

As Nerita had expected, there was a big foot-warmer and also two fur rugs.

She wrapped Anthony in the rug she had brought with her until he was like a cocoon. She fastened his woollen cap down over his ears and made quite certain the scarf round his neck would keep out any draughts.

"You will be nice and warm, dearest," she said in a soft voice.

"Make the horses go very fast!" he said.

"That is what they will do."

Nerita found that it was not an idle promise, for the Marquis had every intention of going fast.

They set off over the Park and the snow was deeper than Nerita had expected.

It was like being in Switzerland, she thought, where she had spent a winter with her father and mother and loved every moment of it.

She had learnt to skate extremely well and also to ski a little.

Her father had been an expert, but because it worried her mother for her to be away for long and to travel over long distances, she had concentrated more on skating.

She wondered now if she should suggest to the Marquis that as soon as the lake was frozen hard enough she and Anthony could skate.

Then she told herself that there was no point in asking him. She would just order some skates for Anthony and for herself and hope that everybody would think it was a natural way to behave.

The sun was dazzling on the snow as they moved in an enchanted fairly-land where every branch of the trees was glistening and even the snow over which they traveled seemed to be sparkling with diamonds.

They were now some way from the house, and, seeing it standing majestic and even more beautiful in a white setting than it had seemed when she had first arrived, Nerita could not help exclaiming:

"It is so lovely!"

The Marquis followed the direction of her eyes and replied:

"I agree with you, and not only because it is my home."

"You are very lucky," Nerita said, feeling a pang at the thought of Meridon, which she had lost forever.

"You sound envious."

"Perhaps I am," she admitted. "A home is what we all want, and without it we have no roots and no background."

"What has happened in your life that you should speak like that?" the Marquis enquired.

Nerita realised that she had been indiscreet, and she thought too that it was most reprehensible that she should speak to the Marquis as if they had met socially rather than as if he were her employer.

"It is not very . . . interesting, My Lord," she said, and turned to Anthony.

"Now you are just like Father Christmas," she said, "but we have no sacks of toys to give away to the children who are waiting for us."

"Father Christmas had reindeers," Anthony said.

"Perhaps when the reindeer are ill he has to use horses, like we do," Nerita suggested.

"Reindeers are pretty," Anthony replied.

"What I want to know, Miss Graham," the Marquis interrupted, "is how you can play so well and why with such an exceptional talent you chose to take a post as a Nursery-Governess."

"I can explain that quite easily," Nerita said. "A talent is very different from having the genius of *Mademoiselle* Duval."

"*Mademoiselle* was extremely impressed by your playing," the Marquis said. "Before she left this morning she gave me a message for you."

Nerita waited, almost knowing what he would say.

"*Mademoiselle* said: 'Tell Miss Graham that if she comes to Paris I will find her a place in the Theatre, as I promised.' She also left you a small present, which I will give you when we return to the house."

"*Mademoiselle* is very kind," Nerita murmured.

"I feel I owe you more than I can possibly express in words," the Marquis said, "because without you the evening would have been a disaster."

"I am sure *Mademoiselle* could have recited her act without music."

"That is something she would not have done," the Marquis replied. "She expects perfection and the music is very much a part of what she feels and portrays."

"I realise that."

"Then, as I have already said, I am deeply grateful."

Nerita did not reply and after a moment the Marquis went on:

"I felt last night that you should have met my friends who were applauding you and Désirée Duval, but I did not—wish you to join us."

"Of course not," Nerita replied. "I quite understand that. After all, I am only one of your servants."

"I did not mean it that way," the Marquis said, "as you are well aware."

There was something in the way he spoke which made Nerita draw in her breath, and almost defiantly she asked:

"Then what did you . . . mean, My Lord?"

"I mean that you are unique—somebody I never expected to find in my house—or anywhere else—and I was afraid that if you joined my other guests you might—change—and perhaps seem—ordinary."

He spoke as if he was finding it difficult to put into words what he wanted to express.

His eyes were on the horses he was driving, and yet Nerita felt as if he were looking at her, looking deeply into her for the words he needed.

"I think, My Lord," she said after a moment, "that last night we were all . . . carried away by the . . . magic which . . . emanated from *Mademoiselle* and only from . . . her."

"That is not strictly true," the Marquis said, "and I find your mock-modesty, Miss Graham, quite unnecessary."

Nerita glanced at him sharply.

There was a note of cynicism in his voice that had not been there before, when she had felt that he was entirely sincere in what he said.

Now she was not certain.

After a moment she said:

"I think sometimes things happen in our lives which take us . . . out of . . . ourselves. We see things in a different . . . perspective. That is what happened last night. Now we are . . . back once more with the . . . commonplace."

"You are sure of that?" the Marquis asked.

"Quite sure."

"Then if that is true—why are you here?" he enquired.

There was no need to elaborate what he meant and Nerita did not pretend not to understand.

Aloud she replied:

"I wanted to think . . . I wanted to . . . believe that you thought it would give your son . . . pleasure to ride in a sleigh."

"But you know quite well that that was not the reason for my invitation."

Nerita did not answer and they drove on for some while in silence.

She was thinking that this was a kind of conversation in which it was quite wrong for her to be taking part, seeing that he was her employer and remembering the position she occupied in his house.

And yet if she was honest with herself she knew that this conversation was different, although superficially it might appear to be similar, from those she had had with the Italian noblemen who had taken her riding in Rome.

They had flattered her with every word they spoke and with every look they gave her.

This conversation, judging from those which she had previously experienced, was not a flirtation but something more subtle; and there was something too which told her it was far more dangerous.

Despite her resolution, despite her belief that she disliked the Marquis and hated his treatment of Anthony, she felt herself respond to him in a manner which she could not describe.

She only knew that she was vividly conscious of him beside her, and of the broadness of his shoulders, the carriage of his head, and the manner in which he turned his face every so often to look at her.

'It is because he is so overpoweringly masculine,' she thought, and knew that never before had she herself felt so overwhelmingly feminine.

"Why did you come to Wych Park?" he asked, breaking the silence that had seemed to last a long time.

"I wanted employment."

"That is hard to believe when I imagine that the wages I pay you are very small in comparison to the value of the coat you are wearing!"

'So he *has* noticed what I am wearing!' Nerita thought.

Aloud she said:

"My coat was a present."

"That is what I surmised," the Marquis said.

There was a dry note in his voice and a twist to his lips, which made Nerita suddenly angry.

"If you are thinking what I imagine you are thinking, My Lord, it is untrue!" she said sharply.

"So you can read my thoughts just as I can read yours!" he exclaimed.

She was still, and he went on:

"You hated me after the way I spoke to you in the stable, when I thought the child had been hurt. You were still disliking me when you came onto the stage last night and I thought it was impossible for you to accompany Désirée Duval. Now, although I may be mistaken, I think that what you are feeling is different."

Nerita was astonished.

He was not only far more perceptive than she had ever imagined he could be, but she had not expected for one moment that he would be attuned so closely to her that, almost as her father had been able to do, he was aware of her thoughts and feelings.

"I am right?" the Marquis asked after a moment.

"I have a feeling that Your Lordship's interest in a Nursery-Governess is quite . . . unprecedented," Nerita said repressively, "and something which . . . should not . . . happen."

The Marquis laughed.

"If you want to act a part," he said, "I cannot stop you from doing so, but equally you cannot prevent me from speculating as to what is the mystery that surrounds you and why, looking as you do, you should wish to play 'Cinderella.' "

He paused to glance at her, then he said with a smile that seemed to illuminated his face:

"Whatever the reason, may I tell you that I am delighted, intrigued, and extremely curious as to why you should have chosen Wych Park in which to assume such a role!"

Chapter Five

Nerita felt that there was nothing she could say.

She therefore busied herself once again with talking to Anthony.

They were passing some stags, which, alarmed by the sleigh, trotted away from them, and he was excited and wanted to follow them.

They drove on, until quite suddenly the sunshine vanished and it started to snow.

The Marquis looked up apprehensively at the sky.

"We must turn back at once," he said. "I think we are going to have a heavy storm."

He found, however, that it was unwise to turn back until he reached a piece of flat ground on which he knew the horses would not be bogged down.

Even as they started on the homewards journey the snow fell more heavily, and there was also a wind which blew it in their faces.

Anthony began to whimper and Nerita put her arms round him and drew him close against her.

"We will soon be home," she said optimistically.

But she knew as she spoke that the horses were slowing down because it was extremely difficult to see, and the Marquis was forced to drive at little more than walking-pace.

Nerita bent her head, finding that the snow-flakes whipping against her cheeks hurt her and being almost blinded because they rested on her long eye-lashes.

She had the idea that the horses were suffering from the same difficulty.

Anthony, pressed against her, began to protest.

"I'se cold!" he said. "I want to go home!"

"We are going home now," Nerita said soothingly. "The horses are finding it hard to go quickly with the snow in their faces. You do not like it, nor do they!"

"I'se cold!" Anthony repeated petulantly.

Nerita thought he was not so much cold as bored and uncomfortable, but she was helpless to do anything about it, and as she looked at the Marquis as if in appeal, he said:

"I cannot believe the violence of this storm will continue for long. We will try and turn into the wood, where the trees will afford us some protection at any rate."

He turned the horses to the right as he spoke, and after a few minutes of being unable to see anything ahead of them there was suddenly the faint outline of trees.

It took the Marquis a little time to find a break in them, but eventually they drove along a narrow track with trees on either side.

"I have just remembered that there is a wood-cutter's hut a little farther on," he said. "Perhaps it would be best for you to shelter there."

"It is a good idea," Nerita agreed; "and, as you say, the snow is so heavy that I cannot believe it will continue for very long."

"We can hope not," he replied.

A few minutes later he drew the horses to a standstill and Nerita saw that he had been right, for there was a wood-cutter's shed just ahead of them in a clearing where men must have been working quite recently.

The Marquis drew the horses as near to the shed as he could, then he said:

"Do not move. The snow is deep and I will carry you over it."

The horses stood quite quietly while he attached the reins to the buckboard and stepped out. Then he held out his arms and Nerita moved Anthony from beside her towards his father.

He was still protesting that he wanted to go home, but the mere novelty of leaving the sleigh silenced him and Nerita saw him put his arm round the Marquis's neck as he carried him towards the hut.

She folded the fur rug which had covered him, thinking that it would be wise to take it with them.

Then she was just going to step down into the snow, hoping that her kid boots were high enough to prevent her legs from getting wet, when the Marquis came back.

"Will you take the rug?" she asked.

"I will take you first," he replied.

"I can walk," Nerita said quickly.

"Nonsense!" he answered. "The snow is very deep."

She thought it would sound foolish to protest. At the same time, she felt shy at being in the Marquis's arms.

Then she told herself that he would behave in exactly the same way to any woman he was with, whether she was six or sixty.

Putting the rug down on the seat, she stood up and let him lift her out of the sleigh.

She wanted to apologise for being any trouble, and yet somehow the words would not come to her lips. Instead, she felt a strange sensation at being close against him and feeling the strength of his arms.

It was a sensation which was different from any that she had ever felt before, but she told herself that she was being nonsensical.

She was no closer to the Marquis than she would be to any man with whom she was dancing.

And yet it now seemed very different, and she was vividly conscious that his face was near to hers, and, as she had thought when he was driving, he was overwhelmingly masculine.

It was only a few steps to the hut and he carried her to the door and set her down on her feet.

"I will fetch the rug," he said, and left her in a manner which she felt was somehow needlessly abrupt.

Anthony rushed towards her.

"This is a funny little house," he said. "Perhaps this is where the three bears live."

"It might easily be," Nerita agreed, "but they are not at home now."

The hut was well made with split logs. There was a small window and Nerita saw a rough fireplace which the woodmen obviously used when it was very cold.

There were thick grey ashes from previous fires and in one corner of the hut there was a pile of small split logs together with some dry grass and withered leaves.

"We can light a fire," she said aloud, "so at least we shall not be cold."

"I'se cold!" Anthony insisted, now that the idea had reoccurred to him.

"Flap your arms together as you have seen the workmen do," Nerita suggested. "You will soon get warm."

Anthony had no wish to exert himself, however, and as the Marquis returned carrying not only the rug and the foot-warmer but also the cushioned back of the sleigh, he rushed at him, saying:

"Light a fire. I want a fire!"

"Give me time," the Marquis replied good-humouredly. "I have to see to the horses first."

He put down the things he was carrying, smiled at Nerita, and went out again.

She thought there was something robust and strong about him, and she was quite certain that whatever the weather was like it would not perturb him.

She knew that had he been alone and unhampered by her and Anthony, he would have driven on home, however bad the storm might be.

She picked up the foot-warmer from where the Marquis had laid it, and, setting it down near the fireplace, told Anthony to sit on it.

Then as she propped the cushioned back of the sleigh against the nearest wall she realised that the ground was dry, and soft from long usage. They would be quite comfortable sitting in front of the fire once it was lit.

The Marquis returned and she saw that the snow was thick on his shoulders, and he shook it from his tall hat before he entered the hut.

"It hardly seems possible," he said, "but the snow is worse than ever!"

"Will the horses be all right?" Nerita asked.

"They are sheltering under the branches of the trees," he said, "and I am certain that as they stay at Wych Park all the year round, they are far more hardy than those I have in my stables in London."

"They are all exceptionally fine," Nerita said. "I find myself admiring them more every time I see them."

"I thought you would appreciate good blood-stock," he said, and she wondered how once again he was so perceptive about her.

Anthony was determined not to let the Marquis's attention wander from his own needs.

"A fire!" he cried. "Make a fire so we can warm our hands."

The Marquis fetched some of the dry grass and leaves from the corner and laid the spare logs on top of it.

Nerita watched him and as the fire flared into life she said:

"You are certainly very proficient at fire-making!"

"I was at Eton," the Marquis replied. "If there is one thing a public-school teaches one, it is to be able to light a fire. Fags get beaten if their fires go out."

There was a little smoke to begin with, but the woodmen had constructed their hut with a view to their own comfort and soon the logs were burning.

They quickly gave out a warmth which made even Anthony draw a little away from the fire, over which he had been crouching, to sit down beside Nerita.

"Shall we have to sleep here all night?" he asked.

She put her arm round him and drew him close to her so that he could lean back against the cushion.

There was no need for the foot-rest, and when she covered Anthony with the rug he looked like a small dormouse peeping out over the fur.

"I hope not," she replied quickly.

The idea was startling, and she looked at the Marquis. As if to answer her question he went to the window and rubbed the glass with his hand.

"It does not seem to be abating yet," he said, "but it is still a long time to nightfall."

"Not so very long," Nerita argued. "Is it likely that anyone will come and look for us?"

"I imagine they would not think it necessary until after four or five o'clock," the Marquis replied.

Nerita gave a little sigh, but she did not say anything aloud, for fear of frightening Anthony.

However, the small boy seemed quite happy to cuddle against her and watch the fire.

She loosened his coat a little round his neck, and because she personally felt quite hot she slipped back the hood on her own head and tidied her hair with her free hand.

As she did so, she looked up and saw that the Marquis was standing by the fire, and the expression in his eyes made her once again feel overwhelmingly shy.

As if he suddenly made up his mind he said:

"It is impossible for me to stand upright in this hut. I think I would be more comfortable if I joined you. Can you spare me a little of your cushion to lean against?"

"Yes, of course," Nerita replied, trying to speak in a natural tone. "There is plenty of room."

The Marquis took off his overcoat, shook off what remained of the snow, threw it down on the ground, and then lowered himself beside her.

It meant that they were once again very close to each other, and almost as if for protection she turned her head towards Anthony.

"I did not mean this to happen," the Marquis said, "but now that it has, I find it quite an adventure."

"It will not be so enjoyable if we have to stay the night," Nerita replied lightly. "In an hour or two we shall all begin to feel hungry and doubtless thirsty."

"That is a mundane manner in which to look at what may prove to be an exciting story to tell your grandchildren, Miss Graham," the Marquis said with a note of amusement in his voice.

"It is much more likely," she replied without

thinking, "to be a story to please the gossips, if they ever get to hear of it."

She did not look at the Marquis but she knew that he was smiling.

"So you are afraid of being compromised, Miss Graham?"

"I feel sure that Anthony will prove a most adequate Chaperon," she retorted.

Again she told herself that this was not the way she should be speaking with her employer.

But, in some manner which she could not explain to herself, the Marquis seemed to sweep away the natural barriers there should have been between them and even override her instinctive defences against him.

"Tell me about yourself," he said after a moment.

"You must be aware that I have no wish to do anything of the sort," she replied.

"Why not? Most women are always ready to talk about themselves, and I can see no point in your being so irritatingly mysterious."

"If it irritates you, why not dismiss the problem of me from your mind?"

"That is something I am unable to do. I have found myself thinking about you ever since we first met."

"You were certainly irritated then!"

"I was also, when I had had time to think, extremely curious."

Nerita did not speak, and after a moment the Marquis went on in a low voice:

"I was of course aware that you were in the house, but I did not think that our second meeting would be so dramatic. When Mrs. Wilton told me you played the piano well, I expected the usual Drawing-Room performance of an enthusiastic amateur."

"That is what I am."

"Nonsense! You know quite well that you play like a professional."

He paused and looked at her as he asked:

"Is that what you are? A professional pianist who for some secret reason has for the moment forsaken the stage?"

"To keep you amused, or should I say irritated," Nerita replied, "it would be best for me not to answer that question."

"But I will answer it," the Marquis said. "I do not believe that that is the truth, because you look so young; and I cannot quite understand how Marriott was persuaded to engage you."

He waited, then he asked:

"Did you lie about your age? I have a feeling that you did so because you wanted the situation."

Nerita thought he was far too clever and intuitive, and because she did not wish him to probe any further she said quickly:

"I am bored with this subject. Suppose I am impertinent enough to ask you to talk about yourself?"

"That is something I should find very boring."

"Then perhaps it would be best for us both to sit silently and enjoy the warmth."

The Marquis turned his body so that he could look more directly at her.

"If you do not wish to talk to me," he said, "I shall talk to myself. I want to say aloud how beautiful you are, and yet that does not really describe your face, which has so much more than beauty in it."

Nerita turned her head to one side so that all he could see was the tip of her ear.

"That is not a proper way for the Marquis of Wychbold to address his Nursery-Governess," she said coldly.

"I am not concerned with the Marquis of Wychbold," he replied, "but with a man who finds himself alone in very strange circumstances with a fascinating, intriguing creature who might have stepped straight out of a fairy-tale."

"We are not alone," Nerita corrected him hastily.

Then as she looked down at Anthony she realised that the small boy cuddled against her was sound asleep.

The long drive and the heat of the fire after being so cold had naturally made him sleepy.

"I am right," the Marquis said softly. "We are

alone and there is no-one to overhear the things I want
to say to you."

"You must not say them," Nerita said swiftly.
"Please."

She turned her head pleadingly and realised as she
did so that his face was closer than she had expected.

She looked into his eyes and was lost.

She could see nothing but the light in them, which
seemed to reflect the flames of the fire.

She drew in her breath. At the same time, she was
aware that something was happening to her that had
never happened before in her whole life.

She was not even quite certain what it was. She
could not put it into words, and yet it was happening.

She was spellbound by a man she had only just
met, whom she had thought she hated, and yet already
he was a part of her life, of her, of her thoughts.

It seemed as if the Marquis too had been frozen
into a strange stillness.

Then, as if it was inevitable, as if it was part of
their very breathing, slowly his arm went round her
and with his other hand he lifted her chin and his lips
come down on hers.

It was a movement of pure poetry, of music.

It was part of the very beating of Nerita's heart,
and she knew that this was what she had always wanted
and what she knew was waiting somewhere for her in
the world, if only she could find it.

She felt the Marquis's mouth hold hers captive,
felt the warm insistence of his lips, at first gentle, almost tender, then growing more possessive, more de-
manding.

It all seemed to happen not only to her lips but to
her cold body, which responded as if she were a musical
instrument from which he could evoke an ecstatic
melody that came from the Heavens.

How long that kiss lasted she did not know.

She only knew that she was no longer herself but
his, and he was hers, and they were not two people but
one.

In some strange and inexplicable manner, it was

as if they had found each other through time and were united again after a long separation.

Finally the Marquis raised his head and stared into her eyes.

"How could this have happened?" he asked, and his voice was deep and unsteady. "And yet it has, and I think I knew from the moment I saw you that it was inevitable."

Nerita could not speak. Vaguely at the back of her mind she knew that this was wrong and reprehensible, and yet it did not seem to matter.

She could not even think of the Marquis as someone of importance, a social figure, or as a married man.

He was only a man and she was a woman, and they were alone in the world—a world which existed only between the four wooden walls of the tiny hut in which they sat.

The Marquis's arm drew her a little closer.

"Speak to me," he said. "Tell me what you are thinking."

"I cannot . . . think," Nerita replied in a low voice, "I can only . . . feel."

"As I am feeling," he said, "and, my sweet, could anything be more perfect, more wonderful, than your lips?"

His arm tightened and she knew that he would have kissed her again, but she turned her face away.

"We . . . must not . . ." she began a little weakly.

"It is too late," he said. "Much too late for protests, even for the stirrings of conscience."

He put his fingers once again under her chin and turned her face round to his.

"How many men have kissed you?" he asked, and now she heard a note of very human jealousy in his voice.

"No-one . . . except . . . you."

As she spoke she thought of all the men in Italy who had tried to kiss her, but they were only pale shadows of a past which was long forgotten.

This was real. This was the present. This was what mattered.

The strange rippling thrills going through her because his fingers were touching her chin, because his lips were so near that they were mesmeric.

"I was meant to be the first," he said.

Then he was kissing her again, kissing her with slow, long, passionate kisses which made her heart throb wildly in her breast, and when he released her the breath came quickly between her lips.

His hand touched first her cheek, then her hair.

"How could you be so absurdly beautiful?" he asked. "Your eyes haunt me, and your hair is like no other woman's I have ever seen."

As he spoke Nerita thought that she ought to be jealous of Désirée Duval with her thick, raven-black hair.

Perhaps last night the Marquis had touched it with the same gesture. Perhaps she had stayed in his arms and been far closer than they were able to be at the moment.

Then somehow it did not matter.

It was not just physical possession or physical feelings which united them, but something spiritual and far more fundamental; something that was not of this world and therefore quite inexplicable.

As if once again in some strange way he knew what she was thinking, the Marquis said quietly:

"There is no reason for jealousy. If there have been other women in my life they were only part of my search for you, and now that I have found you they have gone—vanished into the mist—and it is almost impossible for me to remember them."

It was what Nerita felt herself.

Then, as if the talk of other women made her aware that there were also other people in the world, she glanced towards the window.

"We should try to leave," she said.

But the words were merely conventional and there was no wish behind them to do so.

All she wanted was to remain close to him, to know that she was his.

"How can I let you go even for a moment?" he asked. "I want to stay here forever, knowing that there are only two of us in the whole world; an enchanted world which I have never entered before."

It was what Nerita felt herself, and there was a touch of awe in her voice as she said:

"It is . . . enchanted. That is the right word . . . and we too . . . are enchanted."

"You enchant me," the Marquis said. "I think in fact you are not real but a witch, and I have been spellbound since the first moment I saw your incredibly lovely face looking at me with disdain and dislike."

"And now?" Nerita questioned.

He ran his fingers down her small straight nose, softly over both her eye-lids, then outlined the curve of her lips.

It made her quiver with a sensation she had not felt before, and he smiled as he said:

"Oh, my darling, I know everything about you, even though you will not tell me any facts about yourself. I know that I can excite you as you excite me to madness. I know that I can thrill you, that I can awake in you sensations which are, I promise you, intensified every time I touch you."

He kissed her chin and then the corner of her lips as he went on:

"As I am the first man to kiss you, so many other firsts lie ahead of us, and each one more thrilling, more rapturous, than the last."

Again at the back of Nerita's mind something stirred to tell her that she should not listen to him.

What he was saying was wrong, and the fact that they should love each other was but a fantasy that must dissolve when they left the confines of the wood-cutter's hut.

But his fingers were touching the softness of her neck beneath the fur collar, and she knew it was impossible to stop him.

She wanted to kiss him and for him to kiss her with an intensity that seemed to burn through her body like a flame from the fire.

His fingers tightened, holding her neck as if he would throttle her, then he said:

"I want you! God knows, I want you and I cannot contemplate the future without you!"

He was kissing her again, this time more roughly, fiercely, almost violently, until she put up her hands a little beseechingly as if to save herself.

The gesture checked him and his lips released her. Then after a moment he rose to his feet and walked not to the window but to the door of the hut.

He opened it and the cold seemed to come in almost as sharply as a dash of cold water in the face.

The Marquis stood looking out, and watching him Nerita felt a little of the tumult within her breast subside, and it was easier to breathe.

Then he said in a voice that was hard to recognise:

"I will take you back. It is not snowing so heavily. I think we can get through."

She wanted to cry out because they must leave their place of enchantment, the place where they had left behind the world, which now once more was encroaching on them.

As if the cold or their emotions disturbed him, Anthony stirred, awoke, and rubbed his eyes.

"I want my tea."

"You can have your tea soon," Nerita answered in a voice which she tried to make steady and ordinary. "We are going home."

She pulled him to his feet and tightened the scarf and coat round his neck while he stood there sleepily and yawned.

The Marquis had put on his overcoat and picked up his hat, then had gone out of the hut, closing the door behind him.

"We will soon be home," Nerita said, speaking more to herself than to Anthony.

"And what will happen then?" she longed to ask. "Has this all been just an illusion, a dream? A moment when we stepped out of time and found a magic that will never be recaptured?"

She wanted to run to the Marquis, as Anthony might have done, for him to reassure her, to put his arms round her and hold her close against him.

She had the feeling that he was fighting the same battle within himself as she was. For at the moment they were as estranged from each other as they were when they had first met.

She pulled her hood over her hair, remembering how he had touched it with his fingers.

Then she busied herself with putting out the fire by covering what was left of the smouldering logs with the ashes.

It might go on glowing for some time, but it would not be dangerous, and she wondered if that was what would happen to the feelings the Marquis had aroused in her and she in him.

Was the burning brilliant flame that had flashed between them extinguished, leaving nothing behind but a few smouldering embers?

She felt she could not bear it, could not for a moment have entered a very special Heaven only to be turned away into an empty, barren exile.

'I shall never feel like this again for anyone,' Nerita thought to herself.

Then as the Marquis came back into the hut and looked at her, she saw the expression in his eyes and knew that the fire between them was still burning and their enchantment was still with them.

He picked up the cushioned back against which they had leant and the rug and took them outside.

Then, still without speaking, he returned to lift Anthony up into his arms and carry him to the sleigh.

"I love him!" Nerita said to herself. "I love him and I did not know that love could be so overwhelming . . . a meteor . . . a thunder-bolt . . . a flash of lightning that illuminates the whole sky!"

She waited for his return and suddenly he was there.

He seemed to fill not only the doorway but her eyes, her heart, her whole horizon.

Without even meaning to she lifted her face to his.

He pulled her roughly into his arms and kissed her until the world swung round her and she was dizzy from the wonder of it.

Then he picked her up and carried her to the sleigh.

The horses, their backs covered with snow, were standing quite docilely, facing the direction in which they were to leave the woods.

Anthony was tucked round with a rug and Nerita got in beside him, but this time she put him between the Marquis and herself so that he could be protected from the snow and cold.

She thought that the Marquis might protest; however, as if he understood that she was considering the child, he said nothing, but swung himself into the driver's seat and urged the horses forward.

It was still snowing but the violence of the storm had obviously passed.

Now it was possible to see quite clearly the trees on either side of them, and once they were out of the woods and in the open the Marquis made the horses move faster.

Soon they were proceeding at quite a considerable pace back towards the house.

It was nearly dark by the time Nerita could see the faint outline of the great building ahead of them, the lights in many of the windows glowing golden.

She felt as if they brought her a message of hope and of happiness, but quite how and why it could be possible she had no idea. She knew only that she was happier than she had ever been in her whole life.

All the terrible things that had happened to her since her father's death had receded, and all that mattered was that the Marquis was there and she knew without his saying so that he felt as she did.

She was aware that she was still living in the dream-land into which his kisses had taken her. There were problems, perhaps insurmountable difficulties, to be faced, but for the moment they did not matter.

She could only feel as if her whole body was glowing with a radiance of light and she was not human but immortal!

It was love that made her feel like that. Love for a man who did not even know her true name and was married to the mother of the child who separated them in the sleigh.

After they had entered the house it was more difficult than Nerita had even imagined it would be to leave the Marquis in the Hall and walk up the stairs holding Anthony by the hand.

They had stepped back into reality when as they came through the front door she heard the Butler say:

"Lord and Lady Grantham have arrived, M'Lord, and Sir Mortimer Lawrence."

The Marquis was taking off his overcoat and he did not reply, and Nerita did not look at him as she turned away towards the stairs.

They were no longer in an enchanted hut, they were at Wych Park. While the Marquis must go to the Drawing-Room to greet his guests, her place was in the Nursery with the child she was paid to look after.

When finally they reached the landing of the third floor Emily was waiting for them.

"Where have you been, Miss Nerita?" she asked in a scolding voice that told Nerita she was upset and also frightened. "When they told me you'd gone out in a sleigh with His Lordship, I couldn't believe my ears!"

"We would have been back sooner," Nerita answered, "but the snow was so heavy that we had to take shelter."

"You must be crazy to have gone in the first place!" Emily said.

"I was hardly in a position to refuse."

"When one of the footmen told me where you were, Miss Nerita, I thought he must be joking!"

Emily paused for a moment, then went on:

"His Lordship's never been known to pay the slightest attention to Master Anthony for the last six years. Why should he want the child with him now? That's what I'm asking myself."

Nerita led Anthony to the front of the fire and said:

"Please start to undress Master Anthony, Emily, while I take off my own things."

She went into her bed-room and shut the door.

When she had taken off her fur hood and her coat, she sat down at the dressing-table to stare at her reflection in the mirror.

Was she really beautiful as he had said she was? Did she look any different now from the way she had looked before they had driven in the sleigh?

It was impossible to answer the questions for herself, but she thought that her eyes were shining in a strange way, and her lips were soft and red because they had been kissed.

Then she gave a sigh that seemed to come from the very depths of her being.

She had to face facts. She had to acknowledge that the love which transfused her whole body was wrong and would have shocked her mother.

Perhaps, she told herself, her father would have understood. He had said that love was an irresistible force.

It had been a force which made it quite impossible for her to resist the Marquis or to prevent him from kissing her. It had not been a question of whether he should do so. It had just happened because they belonged to each other.

What was more it had seemed right and as beautiful as the stars in the sky or the untouched snow on the ground, and just as pure.

Yet from the world's point of view it was nothing of the sort.

Nerita sat for a long time staring at herself, trying to collect her thoughts, trying to step from the dream-world which still encompassed her back to the commonplace where Emily was waiting to rage at her.

'I cannot bear it!' she thought.

She felt as if something so perfect and yet so fragile was being destroyed by clumsy hands, and she was unable to prevent it.

Her love was like a flower which was growing on the edge of a precipice and which was such a unique and unusual specimen that it would be worth endangering life itself to possess it.

Even so, it could be destroyed by the roughness

of the winds or a storm. Then she might never find it again.

If was an agony that she had never envisaged in her whole life to sit alone on the third floor of the great house and know that far away below her the Marquis was entertaining his friends.

He would be offering them refreshments after their journey, hearing the latest gossip from London, and perhaps being glad to see Lady Grantham, who had once meant a great deal in his life.

It was her children's pony, Robin, that Anthony rode, and yet when her children had stayed here while she was what Emily called a "close friend" of the Marquis, her little girls had not played with Anthony.

Why?

Why, if he had been infatuated with her and she had been his mistress, had the Marquis not talked to her about his son?

Neither had he done so, Nerita thought, to her.

She now realised that he had never spoken directly to the child, nor, when he referred to him, had he said "Anthony," or "my son."

"He hates him!" she told herself simply. "Perhaps one day he will tell me why. In the meantime, I will remember that Anthony's mother is still his wife."

She rose from the dressing-table to stand at the window and look out into the gathering darkness.

It had stopped snowing and the uncurtained windows had turned patches of the snow to gold. Beyond them there was only darkness.

The gold was the love that she had found unexpectedly and yet so vividly that it possessed her utterly. The darkness was the difficulties which encompassed the Marquis's life and her own.

She had almost forgotten in her preoccupation with him that she was a social pariah, somebody who could not use her own name for fear of what people would say.

Doubtless the Marquis and his friends were among those who had lost money, perhaps great fortunes, because they had followed her father—Dashing Dunbar.

That was another insurmountable barrier that lay between them.

Down below, the housemaids were drawing the curtains in the lighted rooms, for suddenly one patch of gold on the snow disappeared and then another.

Nerita thought with a sudden throb of her heart that it was symbolic.

She had found the perfection of love. She had found what only a few very fortunate people find in their lifetime—the other half of themselves.

But between her and the Marquis there were two insurmountable barriers.

Even as she thought of him she had a sudden fear, almost a dread, that he might ask her to be his mistress! After all, what else was there that he could offer her?

She knew that not only because of her upbringing but because to accept such a position would defame the memory of her mother, she must refuse him.

To accept would debase the love they had for each other.

It was not just a physical need that could be assuaged because their bodies were satisfied.

It was something so very different, so much part of the Divine, that to spoil anything so perfect would be like destroying the flower she had envisaged growing on the edge of a precipice.

"I shall have to go away," she told herself.

The agony of the decision was a sword piercing not only her heart but her soul.

Chapter Six

After a sleepless night Nerita rose and saw that it was a dull day, misty, with a sullen grey sky.

She saw that it had begun to thaw in the night, for already on the drive the snow looked slushy and with none of the dazzling brillance of the day before.

She had slept very little, at one moment feeling again the rapture and wonder of the Marquis's lips, and the next moment telling herself despairingly that the sooner she left Wych Park the better for them both.

She was certain that he was feeling the same as she was, elated and then depressed, excited and then miserable, but grateful because they had known if only for a brief moment a wonder and a glory that was indescribable.

She helped Anthony dress and he chattered away while they were finishing breakfast, talking of the sleigh-ride the day before, forgetting, now that it was all over, everything but the excitement of it.

"I want to see Robin," he said as he put down his mug.

"I will take you riding," Nerita promised, "and I think that today you might ride in the Park."

Anthony gave a whoop of joy and Nerita did not explain that because the snow was thick she thought that if he did fall off he would be very much less likely to hurt himself than if he fell on hard ground.

She was sure that the Marquis would be busy with

his friends, and she had learnt from Emily that there
had been a big dinner-party last night.

She therefore thought she was safe in going early
to the stables, and Anthony was as usual in a frantic
hurry to get to his pony.

Dawkins, the Head Groom, greeted them with
surprise.

"Oi wasn't expecting ye so early, Miss."

"I thought it would be a good idea for Master Anthony to have his ride while it was fine," Nerita replied.

The Head Groom looked up at the sky.

"Looks more like fog than snow, Miss," he said.

They walked towards the stall where Anthony was
already patting Robin and waiting impatiently for the
pony to be saddled.

"I thought Master Anthony might ride in the Park
today," Nerita suggested. "He has been longing to do
so for some time and the snow is thick on the open
space beside the drive."

This was a part of the Park which bordered on a
drive which divided from the main one and led towards
another gate situated on the west side of the Estate.

"Oi'll come with you, Miss," the Head Groom
said. "Oi'll tell one of the stable-lads where Oi can be
found, if His Lordship wants Oi."

They set off a little while later, Anthony shouting
for joy at the thought of riding in the open, the Head
Groom good-humouredly taking him at a trot, while
Nerita followed sedately behind.

She had put on the highest boots she possessed but
she found when they reached the Park that she had to
walk carefully, otherwise the snow, which was very
deep, would go over the top of them.

Anthony was in his element as for the first time he
was allowed to ride by himself without a leading-rein.

"He rides well," Nerita said as they watched him.

"Ye'll soon have t' accompany him on horse-back,
Miss, otherwise he'll get away from ye," the Head
Groom replied.

With a little pang of her heart Nerita remembered that this was what she had longed for.

Now, she thought, it was too late. Anthony would soon be able to ride all over the Estate, but she would not be there to accompany him.

There was no doubt that the child was likely to become an accomplished rider and she wondered if before she went away she should suggest to Dawkins that he should have a pony of his own.

She could imagine that nothing would upset him more than that Lady Grantham should decide to take her children's pony away while the Marquis was not prepared to give his son a replacement.

The words were almost forming on her lips when she was aware that travelling along the drive towards them there was a closed carriage with a coachman and a footman on the box.

She thought it was too early for anyone to be calling and wondered if perhaps it was another guest arriving to join the Marquis's house-party.

Then the carriage was drawn to a standstill and though it was too far away for her to see clearly she thought she could see the vague outline of somebody staring out through the carriage window.

The Head Groom had told Anthony to ride round them in a circle, which was what he was doing, but all the time he was urging Robin to go faster, although the fat, rather lazy pony had no intention of over-exerting himself.

Nerita turned her head to watch the child and suddenly to her surprise she saw that the footman who had been on the carriage had alighted and crossed the snow and now stood beside her.

"Excuse me, Ma'am," he said, "but a lady'd like to speak with you."

Nerita glanced over her shoulder in surprise.

Then, thinking that it must be Lady Grantham who was in the carriage and the communication would concern the pony, she turned and walked through the thick snow towards it.

The footman hurried a little ahead of her to open the carriage door.

Nerita looked inside and saw a lady swathed in furs.

"Will you get in?" she asked. "The cold is bad for me."

She spoke in rather a weak voice, and because Nerita could not very well refuse she stepped into the carriage.

"Will you sit down?" the lady said.

Nerita did as she was asked, at the same time noticing that the occupant of the carriage did in fact look very ill.

Her face was painfully thin, making her eyes seem very large, and yet she was still beautiful, or perhaps the right word was "glamorous."

Nerita noticed that the furs were superlative and so were the large pearls round her neck and in her ears.

She wore a bonnet trimmed with purple feathers and there was a bunch of parma violets pinned on her shoulder amongst the sables.

"Who are you?" the lady asked.

"I am the Nursery-Governess to the little boy on the pony. He is Lord Burton, son of the Marquis of Wychbold."

"Yes, I know," the lady said, "and that is why I wished to speak to you."

A sudden thought struck Nerita and as she stared with a startled expression in her eyes, the lady said:

"I think you have guessed. I am that little boy's mother!"

Nerita drew in her breath.

So this was the Marquis's wife! This was Anthony's mother, who had run away and left him!

She found it impossible to think of anything to say, and after a moment the Marchioness went on:

"I have longed to see my son. I have begged and pleaded with my husband to send him to me if only for a short visit, but he has always refused. So instead I have had to come here myself."

"Does His Lordship . . . know?" Nerita questioned, hearing her voice stammer.

The Marchioness shook her head.

"What would be the point of telling him? If I had done so, he would somehow have prevented me from seeing Anthony. That is why I am going to ask you to be very kind and bring him here to talk to me."

She saw the indecision in Nerita's face and added quickly:

"I think you will understand when I tell you that I am dying."

Nerita looked at her incredulously.

"It is true," the Marchioness said softly, as if she had been asked a question. "I have a very little while to live. The Doctors have told me the truth, and you will understand that I want, if only for a few seconds, to hold my son in my arms before I die."

There was something in the way she spoke which brought tears to Nerita's eyes.

"I will fetch Anthony," she said simply.

She made a movement as if to leave the carriage, but the Marchioness put out her hand to prevent her.

"Tell me about Anthony," she pleaded. "Is he happy?"

"Everything is done for his comfort," Nerita replied, "but he is a very lonely child, and he lacks the most important thing in the world—his mother's love."

Even as she spoke she thought perhaps it was a cruel thing to say, and yet she could not forgive a woman who had left her child when he was only a baby and had managed without him for six years.

"That was what I feared," the Marchioness whispered.

The way she spoke made Nerita wish she had not been so blunt.

There was silence for a moment, then the Marchioness added:

"Please fetch him here. Tell him I have a present for him. He need not know who I am, and I will not keep him long since I have a train to catch.

Without saying anything Nerita knocked on the window, and instantly the footman who was standing outside opened the door.

She stepped out into the snow and hurried to where Anthony was still riding round and round.

"Faster! Faster!" he was crying to Robin, and his

eyes were bright and his cheeks pink with the exercise.

She reached him and put her hands on the pony's bridle.

"I have not finished my ride!" Anthony said quickly.

"No, you shall go on riding," Nerita replied, "but there is a lady who wishes to speak to you in the carriage over there. She has a present for you."

"A present?" he queried.

Nerita knew he liked presents, and she added:

"A very nice present. Something you wanted."

"Shall I ride to her?" Anthony asked.

"Yes, of course," Nerita agreed.

She turned Robin's head in the right direction and Anthony set off so quickly that she had difficulty following him.

She saw, however, that Dawkins, aware of what was happening, was hurrying towards them.

Anthony rode to the drive and the footman lifted him from the saddle and put him through the open door of the carriage.

Nerita reached the pony a moment later and took hold of his reins.

"Thank you," she said to the footman.

She led the pony a little way from the carriage, not wishing to intrude or indeed seem curious about this long-delayed meeting between a mother and her son.

She wondered what the Marchioness would think of Anthony.

He certainly did not resemble her in any way, but then it was difficult to envisage what she looked like before becoming so ill and emaciated.

It was easy to see that she had been beautiful, but she did not have the dark eyes that were such an outstanding feature of Anthony's face, nor indeed his rather sallow skin, which was characteristically Italian.

The Head Groom joined her and took the pony's reins from her.

"There is someone here who has a present for Master Anthony," Nerita explained. "He was very good and did not mind giving up his ride for a few minutes."

"Oi ought to be a-getting back to th' stables, Miss," the Head Groom said.

"Then you go," Nerita replied. "Master Anthony will be all right with me."

"Oi don't like leaving ye alone, Miss, but Oi'll tell ye what Oi'll do. Oi'll send one o' me lads in case ye gets into any difficulties."

"We will not do that," Nerita said with a laugh. "The only difficulty will be to make Master Anthony give up riding, and that argument usually starts when he has reached the stable-yard."

Dawkins agreed.

"Fair dotes on that pony, he does, an' that's a fact."

Nerita was just going to discuss the idea of Anthony having a pony of his own when she remembered that the Head Groom was in a hurry to get back to the stables.

She supposed that the Marquis might be sending for carriages or horses for his guests.

She wished with all her heart that she could put the clock back to yesterday, with the prospect of driving with him in the sleigh.

She drew in her breath at the memory, living again that moment when she had turned her head to look at him in the wood-cutter's hut and their lips had found each other's.

'The force of love,' Nerita thought to herself.

Nothing and nobody, she thought, could have prevented the Marquis from kissing her or from her responding to him.

She was deep in her thoughts, so that a sound behind her did not immediately penetrate her mind. When it did, she looked back to see that the carriage with its two horses was driving towards the house.

It occurred to her that the Marchioness had decided after all to see her husband, and Nerita wondered if the Marquis would be angry not only at her intrusion but also that she had been allowed to see Anthony without his permission.

She felt afraid that he might be angry with her. After all, she had taken it upon herself to let Anthony get into the carriage with his mother.

Then when she had decided that the only thing she could do was to lead the pony back to the stables, she saw the carriage returning.

She knew now that her anxiety at the idea of the Marchioness going to the house was quite unfounded, and they had in fact merely gone to the junction with the other drive, where there was room to turn the horses.

She felt with a sense of relief that the Marquis would not after all be subjected to an uncomfortable scene, if that was what it would have been.

At the same time, she thought he ought to know that the Marchioness was dying. Perhaps it would make him relax his attitude towards her and he would give her permission to see Anthony.

Once again she turned Robin in the direction of the drive, expecting the carriage to stop where it had before, but instead it passed her at a good pace.

She thought she had a glimpse of Anthony's face, but then the carriage drove by and as she stared after it in astonishment it vanished into the mist.

Nerita stood in bewilderment, holding the pony, while conflicting thoughts swept through her mind.

Were they perhaps just driving up and down for the sake of the horses? Or was there a more sinister reason?

She had the uncomfortable feeling that the Marchioness had in fact kidnapped her son.

It was hard to believe, and yet, five minutes later when there was no sign of the carriage returning, Nerita knew that that was what had happened.

Leading the pony, she walked as quickly as she could back towards the stables, and while she went she turned over in her mind what she should do.

There were only two alternatives—one, to tell the Marquis what had occurred; the other, to try to prevent the Marchioness from taking Anthony away from the neighbourhood.

She remembered that she had said she had a train to catch.

If only she could reach the station before the train left, she could take Anthony away from his mother and bring him back to his father, where he belonged.

"That is what I must do," Nerita decided.

When she was free of the snow and could move more quickly, she ran down the stable-yard to where the Head Groom was waiting and said:

"I want a carriage please! I have to get to the station!"

"The station, Miss?" Dawkins queried.

Nerita lowered her voice as she replied:

"The lady in the carriage has taken Anthony away with her. I know they are going to the station."

The Head Groom looked at her and Nerita thought that somehow he had guessed the truth but was too good a servant to ask awkward questions.

Instead, in a surprisingly short space of time he had a light travelling-carriage brought from the stables and two horses between the shafts.

They were nearly ready, and the coachman was putting on his tiered overcoat and his cockaded hat, when Nerita thought of something.

"Have you by any chance any money with you?" she asked the Head Groom. "I may have to follow Master Anthony, and I do not want to go back to the house."

Again she knew that he understood.

"Major Marriott's just given Oi one month's wages, Miss. Ye're welcome to it."

"Thank you," Nerita said. "You know I will repay you."

The Head Groom went into the saddle-room and returned a few minutes later with an envelope.

It was heavy with coins and Nerita without even looking at it slipped it into the pocket of her fur coat.

"Thank you," she said again, and stepped into the carriage, which by this time was ready for her.

She heard the Head Groom order the coachman to carry her to the station as quickly as possible, and she was away almost before she had time to question her own impetuosity.

Only as they drove towards the station did she ask herself whether she had done the right thing.

Then she knew that as far as she was concerned it was right to save the Marquis from the embarrassment of arguing with his wife and getting engaged in what might prove to be a tug-of-war between them for their child.

"It would not only upset the Marquis, but it would be bad for Anthony," Nerita reassured herself.

And yet all the time they drove along the country lanes and then along the main highway which led to the station, she questioned her own action in interfering.

The station was much farther from Wych Park than the Halt at which Nerita had alighted when she had arrived with Emily, and when finally the carriage clattered into the yard, she peered out anxiously, hoping to see a train standing at the platform.

"Perhaps it has not yet left," she told herself.

She jumped out of the carriage and ran through the entrance-hall which led her directly onto the platform.

There were several porters standing about and a few passengers who were obviously waiting for a train, but there was no sign of an elegant lady covered in furs or a little boy in his riding-clothes.

She went up to an elderly porter.

"I was hoping to meet some friends," she said, "but they do not appear to be here. Has a train just left?"

"Yes, Miss," he replied, "the Express for Dover."

Nerita felt her heart sink.

"Did you by any chance notice a lady, very smartly dressed, and a little boy?"

The porter thought for a moment.

"Aye, there be a lady, Oi thinks," he answered.

"She wore a bonnet trimmed with purple feathers," Nerita said.

The porter left her to speak to another.

Nerita waited, feeling her heart beating apprehensively.

The two porters came back to her.

"Jeff here remembers a lady an' a little boy," the porter to whom she had first spoken told her.

"Did they take the train to Dover?" Nerita enquired.

Jeff, who was a younger man, nodded.

"There be four of 'em, Miss. I looks after 'em meself. Quite a lot o' luggage they had."

"Four?" Nerita questioned.

"A gent'man as I thought be a courier, 'cause he had the tickets," Jeff counted, "a maid, an' a lady with a purple bonnet, who was holding the hand of a little boy. They gets into a First Class compartment in the front of th' train."

Nerita faced the truth.

She had been right! The Marchioness *had* kidnapped her son!

"Oi'm afraid ye've missed 'em, Ma'am," the older porter said.

"What time is the next train to Dover?" Nerita asked.

"Well, th' slow train should be in anytime now," the man replied. "It stops at every station an' gets into Dover about an hour after th' Express."

Nerita made up her mind.

"Perhaps you would be kind enough to get me a seat," she said.

"Ye'll want to travel 'ladies only', Ma'am? Seeing as ye be alone."

"Yes, please," Nerita answered. "I will get my ticket."

She walked towards the ticket-office but went first outside to tell the coachman to return to Wych Park.

"I expect to be back by the evening," she said, "but I have to go to Dover."

The coachman asked no questions and Nerita thought it would be impossible to give him any sort of explanation or message.

She could only hope that, with his usual indifference towards his son, the Marquis would not realise that neither she nor Anthony was in the house.

She had a feeling that unless he was asked direct questions the Head Groom would be discreet.

There was a quarter-of-an-hour wait before the slow train arrived. When it puffed into the station there were only two First Class carriages.

Nerita, while she felt that it was being extravagant, decided it would add unnecessarily to her anxiety if she had to face the discomfort of a crowded Second Class compartment or an overcrowded Third.

There was nobody in the compartment which the porter found for her, and she guessed that anyone who could afford to travel First Class would automatically have chosen the faster train which was ahead of them.

As the train moved out of the station Nerita settled herself in a corner seat and wondered what chance she had of catching up with the Marchioness before she boarded the boat-train with which the Express obviously connected.

She was vague as to how many Cross-Channel Steamers left Dover every day.

She also tried to remember, having made the journey a number of times in the past, at what time of day they had left.

She had the idea, because it was still early in the morning, that there would be a Steamer a little after midday.

She wondered whether she would have time to follow the Marchioness to the Quay and try to prevent her from taking Anthony with her to the Continent, but she felt that her chances were slim.

The Marchioness, as was to be expected, had a courier with her and also a lady's-maid, and there would certainly be no question of snatching Anthony away by force.

She could only hope that somehow, if she pleaded persuasively, the Marchioness would at least return and discuss with the Marquis her desire to have Anthony with her.

Surely, in the circumstances, if he knew she was really dying, he would not refuse? But it would have been much more sensible to have approached him in the first place rather than take the law into her own hands.

It then struck Nerita that the Marchioness might in fact have told the Marquis of her state of health and he had still not acceded to her request.

There was something very hard and ruthless about him when it concerned his son, and Nerita, although she loved him, felt that in this he was behaving cruelly, in a manner which she wished to believe was alien to his character in every other respect.

"I love him so tremendously," she told herself, "that I want him to have every virtue and to be as fine and noble as my heart tells me he is."

Had he been any different, how could he have evoked a love so perfect, so divine? Surely his character must inevitably be worthy of it.

Because she was thinking so intensely about the Marquis, Nerita did not at first look out the window at the countryside through which they were passing.

Only later, with a start, did she realise that the train was moving more slowly and she saw that outside there was a thick fog.

The Head Groom had been right.

There was not to be any more snow, but the thaw after the winds and bitter cold of yesterday had resulted in fog.

Nerita thought in dismay that she would never catch up with the Marchioness in time. Then she realised that if her train was fog-bound, the same thing would be happening to the Express.

They seemed to be crawling at a snail's pace for the next half-an-hour. Then suddenly with a screech of the wheels they came to a stop.

Now the silence outside was broken by voices and Nerita realised that men carrying flares were walking beside the line.

She opened the window, put out her head, and instantly was assailed by the acrid smell of smoke.

Several more men passed her and now she saw one dressed in the uniform of a Guard.

"What has happened?" she asked.

"There's been an accident, Ma'am," he replied politely.

"An accident?"

Nerita's voice was sharp.

"Yes, Ma'am, there's been a collision between two trains in the fog."

"Was one of them the Dover Express?" Nerita enquired.

"I understand so, Ma'am. I know she was ahead of us."

Nerita opened the carriage door.

"Better stay where you are, Ma'am," the Guard admonished.

"I have friends on the Dover Express," Nerita said, "and I have to see if they are all right."

She saw that the Guard was about to argue, and said firmly:

"The lady who concerns me is the Marchioness of Wychbold. She is travelling with her son, Lord Burton."

She saw that the Guard was impressed, as she had thought he would be.

"If you come with me, Ma'am," he said, "we'll see what we can find out."

The fog was thick—thicker than it had seemed from the carriage window—but there were a number of men with flares and others were joining them.

Escorted by the Guard, Nerita passed her own engine and proceeded a little way down the line.

There was the sharp hiss of escaping steam, but it was in the distance, and the first carriage they came to was undamaged.

They passed the Guard's Van, several coaches containing luggage or livestock, then reached the Third Class compartments.

The first two were still on the rails. The passengers who had occupied them had obviously had a shock, for they were all shouting and clambering out and explaining as they did so what had happened.

Then in the light of the flares Nerita could see the first effect of the collision.

Three carriages were overturned, and as she walked on, the Guard having ordered one of the railwaymen to walk ahead of them, she found complete chaos.

It was hard to see the details but it was obvious that the engine of the oncoming train had hit the engine of the Dover Express head on.

The escaping steam from the two engines was deafening, and the engine which had been travelling west was lying on its side with its wheels still going round and round.

Nerita had eyes only for the First Class carriages, which were in the front part of the Dover Express, and the first one behind the engine appeared to have telescoped into half its original size.

Passengers were being helped or hobbled out of the coaches and laid on the snow-covered verge at the side of the track.

Quite a number of them were injured but obviously still alive; women were crying, children were screaming, and men with blood running down their faces, with an injured arm or leg, were swearing or shouting for medical assistance.

It was all a scene of incredible confusion, made worse by the fact that the lights from the flares seemed to distort every face into something grotesque and fearful.

The Guard made the man escorting them with the flare hold up the light so that Nerita could see quite clearly those who had already been brought from the train.

In the First Class there had been a number of well-to-do passengers—gentlemen wearing coats with Astrakhan collars, women swathed in fur, the jewels in their ears or round their necks glittering in the lights of the flares.

There was no sign of any lady in a purple bonnet, until in the telescoped coach Nerita saw three men carrying with difficulty through the crushed and broken door a woman who she knew at a glance was the one she sought.

The men carried the Marchioness onto the snowy verge and laid her down.

"Not much hope there!" one of them said as he straightened himself. "The roof fell in on her."

Nerita looked down."

She had known even before the man spoke that the Marchioness was dead. Her face was devoid of colour and there was something inanimate about the way she lay with her head at an angle.

Blood had been running down one cheek, but her eyes were closed and it seemed to Nerita that she was at peace and there was no fear in her expression.

Then as the men went back into the carriage she followed them.

"There is a little boy in there," she said. "Please see if you can find him."

They climbed into the wreckage with difficulty. A moment later they appeared not with a boy but with a man.

He was alive and instructing them shrilly to move him carefully because his leg was broken.

There was something unmistakable about the manner in which he was expressing himself and in his appearance that told Nerita he was the courier the porter had thought him to be.

They laid him down beside the Marchioness and Nerita said again:

"There was a little boy in the carriage—a child of six—please see if he is alive."

"That's right," the Guard chimed in. "There's a chance a child might have survived where a grown-up wouldn't."

"There's another woman in th' carriage," one of the men replied, "but she's trapped and I thinks dead. We tried t' move her but 'tis impossible."

"Look for the child!" the Guard said briefly.

It seemed to Nerita as if an hour passed, although it was really only a few minutes, before one of the men shouted and the Guard went to the wreckage to peer inside it.

"We've found him!" Nerita heard one of the men say. "He's pinned under th' seat."

"Get him out!" the Guard said curtly.

"We're a-trying to," the answer came back, "but it won't do no good. He's dead right enough!"

Nerita gave a little gasp. Then when she felt as if

she might faint the Guard put out his hand to take her arm.

"Take it easy, Lady," he said. "There's nothing you can do about it."

"No," Nerita said. "There is . . . nothing I can . . . do."

It was difficult afterwards for her to remember what happened. She only knew that the Guard looked after her in a kindly way.

He found her somewhere to sit, then left her while he sought a Doctor who was moving amongst the casualties and had with him an assistant who was taking down the names of those who were dead and who would therefore be taken to the Mortuary and not to the Hospital.

When the Guard brought him to Nerita's side she managed to explain:

"The . . . dead woman lying in . . . the snow is . . . the Marchioness of . . . Wychbold . . . and the little . . . boy whose body they have not yet managed to . . . get from the wreckage is her . . . s-son . . . Lord . . . Burton."

"Where does Her Ladyship live?" the Doctor enquired.

Just for a moment Nerita hesitated before she replied:

"I would be . . . grateful, Doctor, if you could arrange for the . . . body of the Marchioness and her . . . s-son, Lord Burton, to be sent to Wych Park, where they will be buried."

"I know Wych Park," the Doctor said.

"There's a Halt there," the Guard chimed in!

"Leave everything to me, Ma'am," the Doctor said, "and here is my card."

"I'm sure the Marquis of Wychbold will wish to get in touch with you, Doctor," Nerita said.

"Tell His Lordship that everything will be arranged. If I do not hear from him, the bodies will be carried back in coffins on the first available train to the Halt."

"I am very grateful to you."

"I presume you now wish to continue your journey to Dover?" the Doctor enquired.

"On the contrary, I wish to return to Wych Park," Nerita replied.

"I am sure that can be arranged."

The Doctor looked at the Guard.

"Will you find out what is happening? The line will undoubtedly be blocked for some time."

"I expect that the train this lady has been travelling in will back up to the junction," the Guard replied. "If she changes there, she should get to Wych Halt sometime later this afternoon."

"I am sure you'll be looked after, Ma'am," the Doctor said hurriedly.

The Guard took Nerita to the carriage she had vacated and now she was no longer alone, for people from the two trains that had collided were being packed into the train that would carry them away from the scene of the accident.

Because they had been through a traumatic experience they were all talking shrilly and over-excitedly, the reserve of a lifetime being set aside so that perfect strangers conversed to one another as if they were old friends.

Nerita felt when she was alone that she must break down and cry because little Anthony through no fault of his own had lost his life.

But it was impossible to concentrate on that tragedy when there was such a noise going on round her.

Someone had had the good sense to produce food and drink from the Dover Express.

Although she would never have thought of asking for it, when it was offered to her Nerita accepted a glass of sherry from a prosperous-looking gentleman in a fur-lined overcoat.

A lady who had a picnic-basket which had obviously been filled by a Chef with expensive tastes offered her sandwiches and pastries.

There was a long wait before finally the train backed away from the scene of the accident and, moving very slowly for fear of another collision in the fog, crept back to the junction.

There were trains coming in from a side-line which could carry the passengers who had been on the upcoming train on their journey to London.

Nerita found the Guard and requested that they stop at the Halt for Wych Park.

He immediately acceded to her request, and she knew that her fellow-passengers were impressed when the train drew up at the Halt and the Guard opened the door to help her alight.

She thanked those who had extended her their hospitality, and they wished her good luck in voices which told her that they were wishing her something they felt had been given themselves in not having been injured in the accident.

The fog was by no means as bad at Wych Park as it had been farther down the line.

Nevertheless, as Nerita set out towards the house in the gathering dusk she felt that the sombre mist of the atmosphere was in tune with her own feelings, not only of sorrow for Anthony but also of a fear of the task which lay ahead of her.

"What will the Marquis say?" That was the question which echoed and re-echoed over and over again in her mind.

Even her footsteps in the slushy snow on the road-way, which had melted even more than it had done early this morning, seemed to be saying:

"What will the Marquis say?"

The Halt was on the other side of the small village which lay outside the main gates of Wych Park, and as she was walking towards the thatched cottages Nerita saw a brake from the house standing outside the village shop.

She found a young coachman in charge and when he realised who she was he helped her into the brake, which was used for shopping and for conveying the servants to and from the town, and drove her back to the house.

As they proceeded down the drive Nerita once again

saw the lights in the windows of the great house silhouetted against the darkening sky.

But instead of the elation and the enchanted happiness she had felt the night before when she drove
back in the sleigh with the Marquis, she felt now only
a depression and misery which seemed to encompass
her to the exclusion of all else.

Without asking, the coachman drove the brake not
to the front door but to the one at the side that Nerita
and Anthony usually used when they left the house to
visit the stables.

Could it really have been only this morning that
she had taken the little boy, so excited at the prospect
of riding in the Park, hurrying to the stables because
he wanted to see his beloved pony?

It seemed as if she had lived a century of fear,
anticipation, and horror since that moment.

She thanked the coachman automatically and
walked into the house.

For a moment she hesitated at the stairs that led
up to the Nursery on the third floor.

Then she told herself that she could not speak
to anyone or see anyone until she had told the Marquis
what had happened.

She walked along the passages until she came to
the Great Hall, where she knew there would be a
footman on duty.

There were not only several footmen but also the
Butler, who had been at Wych Park for many years.

He saw her come from the passage and perhaps
something in the expression on her face or his surprise
at her appearance in the front of the house made him
move immediately towards her.

"I have to see his Lordship!" Nerita said.

"His Lordship's playing cards in the Blue Salon,
Miss Graham."

"I must see him ... alone," Nerita said. "It is
... important."

The Butler merely replied with a dignity that was
part of his training:

"Perhaps you'll wait in the Writing-Room, Miss
Graham."

He walked across the Hall, opened the door to a small but exquisitely furnished room with a number of exceptionally fine pictures on the walls, and left her.

Nerita drew off her gloves.

She was conscious of feeling very cold, but when she held out her hands to the fire there seemed to be no warmth coming from the flames and she felt as if all the blood had left her body.

She heard the door open and she drew in her breath, feeling that it was almost impossible for her to find her voice.

The Marquis came into the room and the door closed behind him.

"What has happened?" he asked. "I heard when I asked for you that you had left the house and I could not understand where you had gone, and why."

"That is . . . what I have to . . . tell you," Nerita said.

"You look very tired. Sit down and let me get you something."

"N-no," she said. "You have to listen . . . please . . . listen to me."

He crossed the room to stand beside her.

"What is it?" he asked. "My darling, I cannot bear you to look like this."

Nerita held up her hand. She felt that she might burst into tears at his endearment, and with an almost superhuman effort she said:

"I do not know how to . . . tell you . . . but this morning . . . when Anthony was . . . out riding in the Park . . . a l-lady in a carriage asked to see him."

"A lady?"

"It was . . . your wife . . . the M-Marchioness. She came because she was dying . . . and she wanted to . . . see her . . . son before she . . . died."

Nerita's voice faltered.

She could not look at the Marquis, but she knew that he was staring at her incredulously as if he could hardly believe what he was hearing.

"When Anthony got into the . . . carirage with her . . . they . . . drove away."

"Drove away?"

The Marquis's voice sounded as strange as hers.

"I f-followed them to the station," Nerita continued, "but they had left on the . . . Dover Express."

The Marquis made a strange sound. It might have been an exclamation or an oath. She was not certain which; but because she felt that unless she spoke quickly she would be unable to tell everything that had happened, she went on:

"I followed them in the next train, but in the fog there was a collision between the Express and another train, and when I found . . . them they were both . . . dead!"

She spoke hardly above a whisper but it was as if the last word vibrated round the room.

For a moment the Marquis did not move or speak. It was almost as if he had turned to stone.

Then he walked from her side to stand at the window looking out into the darkness.

After a moment he asked:

"Did you say they were both dead?"

"I have arranged for their . . . bodies to be sent here as soon as possible," Nerita answered. "A Doctor is seeing to it; here is his card. I thought it . . . right that they should come . . . home."

Her voice broke completely on the last word, and now, without waiting for the Marquis to speak or turn from the window, Nerita put the card down on the side-table and went from the room.

Tears were pouring down her cheeks and she began to run.

Ignoring the Great Staircase curving up from the marble Hall, she ran down the passage, finding her way almost blindly to the secondary staircase which led up to the Nursery.

She stumbled up the stairs, still crying.

She reached the Nursery and as she pushed open the door she saw that Emily was waiting for her.

Before the maid could speak, before she could ask the questions which Nerita knew were trembling on her lips, she said through her tears:

"Pack . . . Emily! Pack everything as . . . quickly as . . . possible! We are . . . leaving!"

Chapter Seven

Emily picked up the dishes off the small table and started to carry them towards the tiny kitchen which jutted out at the back of the cottage.

"Shall I help you wash up?" Nerita enquired.

Emily laughed.

"I'll be on my death-bed before I lets you do that, Miss Nerita. And what's there to wash? You haven't eaten enough to keep a mouse alive!"

"I am not hungry," Nerita said, speaking to herself as Emily had already vanished into the kitchen.

Nerita took the white cloth off the table and put it in the drawer, then she went to the window to look out on the sun-covered garden and wonder what she should do with herself this afternoon.

Ever since she had arrived at Emily's cottage in Little Berkhamsted she had found it difficult to fill her time while her thoughts both day and night were with the Marquis.

She had known as she ran up the stairs to the Nursery leaving him in the Writing-Room, that she would not stay at Wych Park while he condemned her for his son's death.

It was her fault that Anthony, who had been in her charge, had been carried away by his mother.

However indifferent the Marquis might be towards the child, Anthony was his son and heir and for six years he had fought every effort on behalf of the Marchioness to take him away.

Now Anthony, with his love of music, with his affection for the pony, was dead!

Nerita knew that he had crept into her heart, and she would have given her own life rather than that the small boy should die in such an unnecessary and tragic manner.

For the Marchioness it was impossible to grieve.

She was obviously a very ill woman and the days of her life were numbered, but for Anthony it was very different.

Nerita did not consider even in her dreams the fact that the Marquis was now free and that it was possible, if he wished it, for him to be married.

From her point of view, feeling as she did about being instrumental in the death of his son, that would be impossible.

As for the Marquis, he had no idea who she was or how unsuitable a wife she would make, with the scandal of her father's bankruptcy and suicide in the background.

For one magical moment, Nerita thought, everything had vanished except the irresistible force of their love, which had propelled them towards each other.

They had known as their lips touched that they belonged to each other in a way that was inexplicable but which transcended any other reality.

"I love him!" Nerita murmured to herself in the darkness of the night.

She felt her whole body vibrate to the strange magical sensations that he had evoked and which were too spiritual, too perfect, to translate into words.

But it had been only a dream—a dream from which she had to force herself awake—and as she cried out to Emily to pack their luggage she felt as if she was propelled from the house by the power of logic and common sense, which superseded everything else.

Without asking too many questions, Emily began to pack.

Their trunks were in a box-room next door to the Nursery and she dragged them out and put in Nerita's clothes so quickly that by the time she had ceased crying and dried her eyes the first trunk was ready to be strapped down.

"If we leave as soon as you are ... ready," Nerita said in a voice that did not sound like her own, "it will be ... easy to pick up a ... train at the Halt."

She knew without having to explain to Emily that the trains had all been delayed by the crash and those that carried the passengers from the afternoon Steamers would be travelling towards London.

Emily stood up and straightened her back, then went to fetch another gown from the wardrobe.

"Where are we going, Miss Nerita?" she asked.

"I have no idea, Nerita answered, "but we have to find ... somewhere."

As she spoke she knew it was immaterial where she went, because when she left Wych Park, her heart, her soul, and her life itself would be left behind with the man she loved.

"I've a suggestion to make," Emily said after a moment.

Nerita raised her eyes to the maid's face, but she was not really interested.

"It might not be very comfortable, Miss Nerita, but I owns a small cottage which is empty at the moment."

"A cottage?" Nerita exclaimed in surprise. "Why did you not tell me before?"

"Well, I only learns about it when we comes back to England, when we were staying with Her Ladyship. To tell the truth, after what happened I'd almost forgotten about it."

"Where is it?" Nerita asked.

"At Little Berkhamsted, not far from London, where my father and mother lived afore they died, and where I was brought up."

"And we can go there?"

"It wasn't their cottage, Miss, it belonged to my Uncle Fred. I always was his favourite, and as I'm the only one of the family unmarried, when he dies he leaves his cottage to me."

"So we can go there at once!" Nerita exclaimed.

"When my brother wrote to tell me about it,"
Emily replied, "he said as how his wife would keep it
clean until I could go down and see it for myself."

"Well, let us go there now," Nerita said. "It seems
almost Heaven-sent at the moment."

She had been thinking that she and Emily might
stay at some cheap Hotel until they found another
position together.

But every nerve cried out against having another
child to care for as she had cared for Anthony, or
being once again a stranger in a strange house.

It had been easier for them to get away from
Wych Park than Nerita had expected.

When they asked for a carriage or a brake to take
them to the station it had come round from the stables
within ten minutes, and if the footman who carried
their luggage down the stairs asked questions of Emily,
Nerita did not overhear them.

They drove away in the darkness and Nerita made
no effort to look back at the house.

Had she tried to do so, she knew, the tears would
have blinded her eyes. Instead, she just sat staring
ahead, her face very pale, a stricken look in her eyes
which Emily knew was shock.

Only as she was changing into her travelling-gown
did Nerita tell her why they were leaving.

"Master Anthony is . . . dead," she said in a
strangled tone. "He and his mother . . . died in a railway . . . accident."

Emily asked few questions, but enough for her to
understand what had happened. Then because she loved
Nerita she ceased to talk of anything but the journey
which lay ahead and the village in which she had lived
as a child.

It was, Nerita thought, exactly what she had expected—a grey stone Norman Church, a village green,
an Inn, a shop, and a few thatched cottages, of which
Emily's was one.

There were two bed-rooms, a Sitting-Room with
ancient ships' beams across the low ceiling, and a
kitchen, which had been added later and in which there
was only room for one person to move about at a time.

It was simple and poorly furnished, but Nerita would have welcomed anywhere if she could be alone and try to think out what she should do in the future.

Because Emily loved her as she had for so many years, she was wise enough neither to scold nor cosset her.

She knew that Nerita was suffering and she was aware that the agony which showed so clearly on her face was not due only to little Anthony's death.

The radiance which had transfigured her after coming from the sleigh-ride with the Marquis, and which had made her so dazzlingly beautiful that even Emily was spellbound by her appearance, had vanished.

Now there was only a dull misery which seemed everyday to intensify as she grew thinner and found it impossible to eat.

Emily came into the Sitting-Room.

"I'm going to the shop to find something that'll whet your appetite for supper," she said. "I'll not be long."

"There is no need to be extravagant," Nerita answered automatically. "An egg will do."

"You had an egg for breakfast, and how much did you eat?" Emily exclaimed. "One spoonful!"

She paused, then went on:

"I do my best, but I suppose what you miss is one of those fancy Chefs to whom your father used to pay a fortune."

Nerita put out her hand impulsively.

"I am sorry, Emily dear," she said. "I am not disparaging your cooking, and no-one could take more trouble, but I feel as if food would choke me, and there is nothing I can do about it."

Emily took her hand and said gently:

"My mother used to say: 'Time heals evertyhing.' You've just got to give it time, Miss Nerita."

"That is what I am trying to do," Nerita answered, "and thank you, Emily, for being so understanding."

"I don't understand," Emily retorted stubbornly, "and I'm not going to try. I just wants to see the colour back in your cheeks and a smile on your lips."

She took her hand from Nerita's and turned away.

"There's a lot I could say," she went on, "but I'm not going to. Is there anything you want from the shop?"

"Nothing I can think of," Nerita replied.

A few minutes later Emily, wearing a black bonnet and her thick cape, walked from the Sitting-Room, carrying a basket over her arm.

Nerita, sitting in a chair by the fire, was pretending to read but the print seemed to dance before her eyes and all she could see was the Marquis's face and all she could hear was the deep note in his voice when he had said:

"My darling, I know everything about you, even though you will not tell me any facts about yourself."

Supposing she had told him? she wondered now as she had wondered a thousand times already.

What would he have said? What would he have felt?

She knew she could not risk seeing the expression in his eyes change, nor to be aware that there was a sudden stiffening of his body.

However much he might have thought that they were enchanted, she was sure that when it came to a qustion of losing a great deal of money, of knowing how his friends had suffered through her father's optimism about the Werzenstein Mine, their enchantment would have faded away.

She had thought that her love was like a flower growing on a precipice, and the cold wind of reality which would have destroyed it quicker than anything else would be the loss of money.

Money in the world in which the Marquis reigned supreme was more important than anything else!

"He must never know," she told herself almost fiercely. "He must remember me as someone who for one minute in time became part of himself and the ecstasy of the Divine."

She felt that she could not live knowing that he looked on her and thought of her with contempt, but she told herself that for Emily's sake if for no other reason she must pull herself together and consider the future.

Her thoughts were interrupted by a knock on the door.

She thought perhaps it was the baker who was calling, and rose to cross the small room and open the door which led into the small garden and then straight onto the narrow road.

She pulled open the door, then stood paralysed into immobility; for facing her was the Marquis!

He seemed almost unnaturally large, with his top-hat on the side of his head and his overcoat making his shoulders appear squarer than usual.

For a moment they just stood there, staring at each other, and it seemed to Nerita that there was nothing to say . . . nothing to explain.

He was there and they had found each other again.

At last he broke the silence as he said:

"May I come in?"

Still it was impossible for Nerita to speak.

She could only move a step backwards, and the Marquis entered the cottage and shut the door behind him.

He threw his hat down on the nearest chair, shrugged off his overcoat, and stood looking at Nerita, who had moved automatically towards the fire as if she needed the warmth of it.

"How could you . . . ?" he began.

Then suddenly—and neither of them had any idea how it happened or even if they had moved—she was in his arms.

He held her and crushed her against him, kissing her wildly, frantically, possessively, as if he could never let her go.

Her lips clung to his and their bodies touched each other's. Everything vanished—problems, difficulties, the cottage itself, the past, and the future.

This was love—love so powerful, so majestic, that everything else sank into insignificance, and there was only love, which carried them into the heights of ecstasy.

At last, when humanity broke under the strain of such rapture, Nerita gave a little murmur and hid her face against him.

"My darling, my precious!" the Marquis said. "How could you leave me?"

His arms tightened as he spoke, as if they told Nerita without words what he had suffered.

"I . . . love . . . you."

"As I love you, and yet 'love' is such an inadequate word. You are mine and without you I am crippled, incomplete."

That, Nerita thought, was what she had felt herself.

"I had to . . . go."

"Why? Why? When I first kissed you we both knew we were one and there could be no life, no existence, apart from each other."

"I . . . thought . . . that . . . it was like . . . dying, to leave . . . you."

"And yet you crept away!"

She thought he was accusing her, and she clung to him. Her heart was singing because she could do so.

"I thought I would never find you again," the Marquis said, and she heard the note of fear in his voice.

"H-how did you . . . find me?" she asked, the words sounding incoherent.

He smiled.

"I was really rather clever," he explained, "but if you had not been here I should have spent the rest of my life searching the world for you."

There was something in the tenderness with which he spoke that brought tears to Nerita's eyes.

She looked up at him and he was kissing her again, kissing her eyes, her cheeks, her small straight nose, and lastly her lips.

'I have to think . . . I have to . . . talk to him,' Nerita thought to herself, but to do so was impossible.

The sensations he aroused in her precluded everything else but the feelings of love, the flickering flames rising as they had done before and which she had thought were part of life itself.

At last, with a superhuman effort she took her lips from his and spread out her hands against his chest to push him away.

"We have . . . to talk," she said, her voice faltering.

"Why?" he asked.

"There is ... so much to ... say."

"And plenty of time in which to do so, now that I have found you."

He still held her against him as he continued:

"I had forgotten how beautiful you are! I told you how you had bewitched me, and I can never escape from your spell."

Nerita thought that what she ought to reply was that he would have to, but instead, because she could not relinquish his arms about her or the closeness of his face to hers, she asked again:

"How did you ... find me?"

"When I learnt that you had left the house I nearly went insane!" the Marquis answered. "I could not believe that you had not left me a note telling me why you were leaving and where you were going."

Nerita hid her face against him again.

"I did not ... wish you to ... know."

"The only thing on the nursery-table," the Marquis went on, "were the wages you had borrowed from Dawkins. How could you have thought of him and not of me?"

"I *was* thinking of you ... that was why I ... left."

"I did not know it was possible to suffer as you made me suffer when I thought I had lost you."

"I am ... I am sorry," Nerita said, breathing deeply, "but I was ... doing what was ... right."

"Right for whom?" the Marquis asked almost sharply. "It was certainly not right for me. I love you, Nerita! I love you as I have never loved any other woman in my whole life! We both know that it is impossible to live without each other and our love."

Nerita made an inarticulate little murmur, and after a moment he said in a different tone:

"But I was telling you how I found you. Marriott told me the name of the Agency through which he had hired you, and the moment the funeral was over I rushed to London."

He felt Nerita quiver at the word "funeral" but he went on without pausing:

"An extraordinary old woman in the Domestic

Bureau told me that Emily had been employed at one time by the Countess de Grey, whom of course I know."

Again Nerita quivered, but this time it was an irrepressible jealousy of the woman who had once meant so much in his life.

She felt the Marquis kiss her hair before he went on:

"Fortunately, she has an efficient secretary who had filed away Emily's home address, and she told me it was where she had gone when her parents were ill. So you see, it was as easy as that. But it might have been very much more difficult."

"I did not . . . want you to . . . find me."

"But why, my precious darling, why? I could understand that you were upset over Anthony's death, but it was not your fault."

Resolutely Nerita moved from the shelter of his arms and he let her go.

She stood looking down into the fire, holding on to the small mantelshelf as if in need of support.

The Marquis's eyes watched her, and there was an expression on his face which no other woman had ever seen.

"I should not have . . . let his . . . mother take him away," Nerita said. "I thought perhaps you might . . . blame me for that."

"I understood it was what had happened, when Dawkins told me how the footman approached you while you were watching Anthony ride."

Nerita raised her eyes as she said:

"I am sorry . . . so very sorry. How could I have guessed they would both be . . . killed in that terrible accident?"

"No-one could have foreseen such a thing," the Marquis replied soothingly, "and you are not to blame yourself."

"But I do," Nerita said. "After all . . . although you never seemed to care for him, he was your . . . son."

There was a sudden silence, then the Marquis said abruptly:

"Anthony was not my son!"

Nerita was so surprised that she stared at him in amazement.

"N-not . . . your son?"

"No," the Marquis said, "and now, my darling, sit down. I am going to tell you what I have never told anyone else. It is only right that you should know. And then, please, God, we will never speak of it again."

She knew by the resolution in his voice that she must obey him, but instead of sitting in the arm-chair she sank down on the hearth-rug.

The Marquis sat in the chair and because the room was so small he was very near to her.

"Seven years ago when I was in Rome," he began, "I fell in love—or thought I did."

Nerita drew in her breath but she did not look at him. Her eyes watched the flames of the fire.

"Camille was English, but her grandmother had been Italian. She was staying with her relations and we met at several parties."

The Marquis paused for a moment as if he was looking back into the past, then he said:

"She was beautiful and quite unlike the other women I had known and been amused by in London."

Again he paused, almost as if he was choosing his words, before he said:

"Because I was an impetuous young fool, when she suggested we should be married at once, I agreed, and we left Rome for a country-house that had been lent to us for the first part of our honeymoon."

Nerita shut her eyes. She could not bear to think of the Marquis loving another woman, marrying her, and then going away with her.

"The night we married," the Marquis continued in a strange voice, "Camille told me that she was not in love with me and never had been, but had married me merely so that I should assume the role of father to the child she was carrying by another man!"

"Oh . . . no!"

Nerita could not help the exclamation which fell from her lips.

"The father, who was already married, was Antonio Cosmillo."

Nerita repeated the name beneath her breath.

Antonio Cosmillo was one of the greatest singers in the world. She had heard him half-a-dozen times when she had been in Rome.

She had also heard him sing in the Opera House in Paris, and once, a long time ago when she was very young, in London.

Now she knew from where Anthony had inherited his musical talent. Now she understood why he looked so Italian.

She could almost see in his dark, eloquent eyes the resemblance to those of Antonio Cosmillo, who had been acclaimed as not only the greatest singer on the stage but also the most handsome.

"I spent my wedding-night alone," the Marquis was saying, "and when we returned to England I found it difficult even to be polite to the woman who bore my name."

He gave a deep sigh, as if he remembered the horror and unhappiness of it.

"Camille found the situation between us as impossible as I did, and as soon as she could travel after Anthony was born, she returned to Rome. There she wrote to me, saying she had no intention of returning but intended to live with Antonio Cosmillo as his mistress. She asked me to send them their child."

"And you refused?" Nerita questioned.

"I refused because I would not admit to anyone the way in which I had been fooled," the Marquis said harshly. "I was ashamed of having behaved like a callow youth, blinded, by my own desire for a beautiful woman, into an impetuous marriage which proved so disastrous."

He hesitated before he went on:

"I was too proud to proclaim what I knew was partly my own fault, and I therefore hurt myself, and incidentally you, my precious."

Now Nerita could understand. Now she knew why he had ignored the child, who was not his but was legally his heir.

Now she realised how much he had suffered in knowing that he was tied for life to a woman who had never been his wife in anything but name.

She was aware of how humiliating it would have been for him to have to sue for a divorce and for the whole sordid story to be made public.

Instead, he had given the child who had been foisted upon him every luxury, but had denied him what was more important to a child than anything else —the love of his parents.

It had been cruel, perhaps ruthless, and yet she could understand, because she knew as perhaps no-one else would have done that underneath his pride the Marquis was vulnerable and sensitive.

For six years he had kept silent—for six years he had suffered!

Because she could not help herself she put out her hand and laid it on his knee.

"I am sorry this . . . happened to . . . you," she said softly, "but now I . . . understand."

"I knew you would, my darling," the Marquis said, covering her hand with his, "and now there need no longer be any secrets between us."

Nerita shut her eyes.

She had forgotten! Now it was her turn to confess; now she could no longer hide her shameful secret from him.

Because it was easier to speak standing up, she rose to her feet.

"No, do not move," she said when the Marquis would have risen too. "I have . . . something to . . . tell you."

He looked at her enquiringly, and she said:

"I cannot tell . . . you, if I am . . . near to you."

She thought there was just a flicker of fear in his eyes that something might yet go wrong, and she continued hastily, because she could not bear the suspense:

"I love you! I love you with . . . all my heart and . . . soul, but I cannot . . . marry you."

She clasped her hands together as she spoke, and, standing in the center of the small room, there was a

tragic expression on her face and in her voice that
checked the words the Marquis was about to speak.

After a moment he said very quietly:

"Having said you love me, and knowing how much
I love you, will you tell me why we cannot be together
as fate has obviously intended we should be?"

Nerita drew in a deep breath.

"My name is not . . . Graham."

"I rather suspected that," the Marquis replied. "I
told you you were Cinderella and I could not imagine
why you should have chosen to hide at Wych Park."

"It was because I wanted to be with Emily,"
Nerita explained. "She was the only . . . person in the
whole world who . . . loved me after my father . . .
died."

She hesitated before the last word, and as if the
Marquis was reading her thoughts perceptively, as he
had done before, he asked:

"Will you tell me who your father was?"

"His name was Dunbar . . . he was known as
'Dashing Dunbar,' and, as I expect you know, he . . .
killed himself!"

Nerita's voice broke on the words, and now she
turned round so that her back was towards the Marquis,
and she put out her hands to hold onto the nearest
chair.

She could not look at his face, could not bear to
see the contempt and perhaps the disgust in his expression, could not watch the gulf between them widen
until it swept them apart and the magic, the enchantment, and the wonder of their love was spoilt forever.

For a moment there was silence.

Then she heard the Marquis get to his feet and it
flashed through her mind that he was leaving—walking
out of her life—and she would be alone, utterly alone,
without him until she died.

Then close behind her, so close that she started
when he spoke, the Marquis said:

"Is that all?"

"Is it not . . . enough? He lost his own fortune and
. . . thousands of people . . . suffered."

"If your father had been instrumental in my losing every penny I possessed, it would not have made the slightest difference. Tell me you know that is true, Nerita, and then I will tell you something else."

He turned her round as he spoke and as she lifted her eyes, fearful and apprehensive, to his, she saw that he was smiling very tenderly.

"How could you think for one moment that money would matter to either of us?" he asked. "We have between us the most valuable thing in the whole world, the most precious, the most perfect—our love, my darling."

He pulled her against him and his lips captured hers.

Now he kissed her with a tenderness which made her cry, and yet his lips were possessive, and she knew that, as he had said, they belong to each other and nothing could separate them.

When he raised his head her eyes were shining through her tears, as if there were a lamp lit within her, and her face was radiant.

"Do you really . . . mean that it . . . does not . . . matter?" she asked.

"I really mean it."

"But I cannot . . . marry you. Think what people would say. They would be . . . horrified!"

"Are there any other people in our lives except ourselves?" he asked. "I love you, and I do not care what anybody else says, thinks, or does. But wait here a moment, my precious one. I have something to show you."

He left her and walked across the room to open the door.

Through the window she could see him pass down the small garden path and onto the road.

Outside, she saw the travelling-chariot he had been driving, which was very fast. It had a hood that could be raised in bad weather, and although drawn by four horses it only accommodated two people with a groom at the back.

She knew that he must have driven down from

London as it was easier to get to the village that way than by train, and she understood his desire for speed because he had wanted to find her.

The Marquis came back into the cottage and she saw that in his hand he carried a newspaper.

"I have a feeling," he said, "that one thing you have been economising on has been the newspapers, or perhaps if you bought one you did not read the financial page."

He opened *The Times* as he spoke, folded back the pages, and held it out to Nerita.

She found it difficult to take it from him, and, as if he understood that she was afraid of the faint hope that was stirring in her heart, he put his arm round her.

He held *The Times* with his other hand while she held it with one of hers.

In headlines splashed across the top of the page she read:

SHARES IN WERZENSTEIN MINE RISE SHARPLY
SENSATIONAL NEW DISCOVERIES ELECTRIFY MARKET
SHARES CLOSE AT NEW HIGH

"It cannot be . . . true!" Nerita exclaimed in a broken voice.

"It is true, my darling. The seam which brought about your father's crash petered out, but somebody who still believed he had been right in the first place dug deeper. There is gold in the Mine—more gold than was at first anticipated. Those who hung on to their shares are delirious with joy."

"I cannot . . . believe it!"

Nerita stared at the newspaper as if she thought it must be deceiving her. Then it was no longer possible to see the words, and the Marquis threw *The Times* on the floor and drew her back into his arms.

"I should have been very proud and happy to marry you, my beautiful love, whoever you might have been," he said. "Even as a bogus Nursery-Governess. But I think it will make you happy to know that your father's luck still holds, and I have the feeling that quite unexpectedly and quite unnecessarily I shall have a very rich wife!"

"The money does not . . . matter," Nerita managed to say, "but I did not want . . . you to be . . . ashamed of me."

"I could never be that," the Marquis answered. "As it is, now we can both face the world without having anything to hide, and we can also start a new life together."

He pressed his lips against the softness of her cheek before he added:

"That is the important word—'together.' And because we know that our love can transcend all difficulties, all problems, we will admit quite simply that it is irresistible, and leave it at that."

There was a touch of laughter in his voice and Nerita looking at him felt as if the whole room was filled with sunshine.

Now the golden light she thought had been denied her was there again.

Now she was no longer in the darkness or in a fog, but enveloped with a radiance which came, she knew, from their hearts and their happiness.

"I love . . . you!"

They were the only words in which she could express the joy which flooded through her like sunshine.

"And I love you, my beautiful darling," the Marquis answered, "not for the moment—not impetuously—but with an unmistakable conviction that nothing else in the whole world is of any consequence except our love."

"Our . . . love!"

Nerita whispered the words.

He looked down at her for a long moment as if he searched deep into her heart. Then he added:

"A love which is a force we can neither control nor alter. It has brought us together and never again can we be separated."

Nerita felt herself vibrate to the note in his voice.

This was the love she had prayed for, the love she had thought she would never find and then believed it was lost.

As if he knew what she was thinking, the Marquis said softly:

"It is true—this is not a dream. I have searched for you all my life, and now, my dearest heart, you are mine as you were born to be."

Nerita's eyes were dazzling as she looked up at him.

"Yours ... all ... yours," she murmured.

Then his lips held her captive and she felt a flame within her leap towards the fire that burnt in him.

It was so perfect, so wonderful, and so overwhelming that she knew the Marquis was right and nothing could ever have kept them apart.

They were one and there was nothing else in the world but the irresistible force of their love.

ABOUT THE AUTHOR

BARBARA CARTLAND, the world's most famous romantic novelist, who is also an historian, playwright, lecturer, political speaker and television personality, has now written over 200 books. She has also had many historical works published and has written four autobiographies as well as the biographies of her mother and that of her brother Ronald Cartland, who was the first Member of Parliament to be killed in the last war. This book has a preface by Sir Winston Churchill. Barbara Cartland has sold 80 million books over the world, more than half of these in the U.S.A. She broke the world record in 1975 by writing twenty books, and her own record in 1976 with twenty-one. In private life, Barbara Cartland, who is a Dame of the Order of St. John of Jerusalem, has fought for better conditions and salaries for Midwives and Nurses. As President of the Royal College of Midwives (Hertfordshire Branch), she has been invested with the first Badge of Office ever given in Great Britain, which was subscribed to by the Midwives themselves. She has also championed-the-cause for old people and founded the first Romany Gypsy Camp in the world. Barbara Cartland is deeply interested in Vitamin Therapy and is President of the British National Association for Health.